FINDING

ELSEWHERE

FINDING
ELSEWHERE

DAVID CADMAN

Editorial & Design Services: The Write Factor
www.thewritefactor.co.uk

Published by Zig Publishing
ISBN 978-0-9566900-4-3

ACKNOWLEDGEMENTS

With thanks to my friend and editor,
Lorna Howarth, and book designer, Rachel Marsh.
Also my thanks to Simone Sandelson for the beautiful
paintings of my hat for the front cover and illustrations,
and to David Gillingwater in helping to translate these
for use within the book.

To my grandchildren,
Felix, Izzy, Lucas, Max and Levi.

CONTENTS

THE WAY OF LOVE

There are principles that govern and lie within all that is, principles that we must understand and live by if we are to be true, if we are to be at one with all that is.

These principles can be discovered in many different ways – through art and music, through philosophy and through studying the teachings of the sages of all time and all traditions, through science, through walking, through gardening, through prayer and through stillness and quietness. Each one of us must find our own way, sometimes on our own and sometimes in company or with the help of a guide.

Some people have called these principles 'God', and some speak of 'Father' or 'Mother', 'The One', 'The Great Spirit', the 'I AM THAT I AM'.

I call these principles 'Love'. For me, Love is.

Those who have studied these things say that we are shaped by the stories we tell each other, and by the stories that are told to us. Indeed, they say that what distinguishes Homo sapiens is the capacity for the telling of stories: stories that bind us together, enabling us to live in tribes and larger groups, eventually becoming part of cities and nations. If this is so, then we have to look carefully at these stories and if we find them to be unsatisfactory, we need to find others. For if we continue to tell stories that are not true we will lose our way.

The stories in this book have come to me over time, sometimes unexpectedly and sometimes in moments of reflection or deliberate thoughtfulness. Increasingly they have come as I have waited in the space between. My muse is Love in all her magnificence and mystery – sometimes tough to know. Some of the stories have been with me for a long time. Others have come to me very recently.

Knowing rests in being aware that we do not know. And as I have become old, it has become increasingly evident to me that I do not know much at all. So, in sharing my stories with you, I am sharing my own 'not knowing', my own adventure.

> Old men ought to be explorers
> Here or there does not matter
> We must be still and still moving
> Into another intensity

T S Eliot, *Four Quartets, East Coker, Part V*

Suffolk, 2015

THE WRONG
TURNING

FINDING ELSEWHERE

THE WRONG TURNING

The King was sitting in his chamber and standing in front of him was a forlorn looking man, the King's Senior Advisor on Calamities and Things to Worry About. He was carrying a thick book, which he had opened at a particular page, and he had begun to address the King.

"I am sorry to have to say this, Your Majesty," he said, "but the findings of our latest report on 'What is Happening' – that is the report prepared by your Majesty's Men in White Coats Who Know Everything – the findings of this report do not offer much comfort. It appears, Sir, that we took a wrong turning."

"A wrong turning," said the King, "whatever do you mean, a wrong turning?"

"Well, Sir," said the forlorn looking man, closing the book and placing it upon a table beside him, "your Men in White Coats are not sure when it was or how it came about, but they now see that some while ago, well, some while ago we took the wrong turning."

"There you go again," said the King, his voice rising with impatience. "There you go, you have said it again. That 'turning' thing, you have said it again. What do you mean, wrong turning?"

The Senior Advisor was now beginning to perspire and took from his pocket a large blue and white spotted handkerchief, with which he wiped his brow. He had begun to feel unwell.

"Your Majesty," he said in a voice that was beginning to creak, "would Your Majesty permit me to sit down for a moment?"

"Sit down?" said the King. "Yes of course you can sit down. Why on earth would I worry if you were standing up or sitting down? Sit down. Sit down."

So the forlorn man, the Senior Advisor on Calamities and Things to Worry About, sat down and tried to recover himself.

"Might I trouble Your Majesty," he said, "for a glass of water?"

"Glass of water?" said the King. "Yes of course you can have a glass of water." And he rang a bell, which summoned a servant in blue stockings and a yellow tunic, who bowed low and asked the King what he would like.

"Bring this man a glass of water," said the King. "And while you are about it, bring me one, too. In fact bring a jug of water and two glasses."

The servant bowed again and left the room, returning shortly with a tray upon which was a crystal jug of water and two glasses. He poured out a glass for the King and then, as was of course right, he poured a slightly smaller one for the Senior Advisor on Calamities and Things to Worry About. For a minute or two neither the Senior Advisor nor the King said anything. The Advisor picked up his book and began to look at one or two of the pages, and the King, with a growing sense that things were not at all as they should be, stared at his shoes, noticing a scuffed patch on one of them.

"So," said the King looking once more at his Senior Advisor, "so what is this 'wrong turning' thing about?"

"Well Sir," said the Advisor now regaining his sense of importance and authority, "we thought it was all for the best. We thought that the more we could make and do, the better it would be for everyone. We thought that all the astonishing things we invented would make life better, richer, more completely wonderful. But I am sorry to say, Sir, very sorry to say, that this latest report by the Men in White Coats is saying that there were things that we didn't take account of. It seems to suggest that we didn't even think about them; that we were not even aware that we might have had to think about them. It was as if they were invisible to us. Not there at all."

The King was beginning to feel rather confused with all the things that apparently had not been taken into account or not even been thought of; things which might have been invisible; and he was also beginning to fear that he was about to be told something very disagreeable, very disagreeable indeed. He took a drink from his glass and looked directly at his Advisor.

"You see," said the Advisor, "we had no idea how warm it might get and how stormy and wet too."

"So is all this 'wrong turning' stuff and the things that you haven't thought of just about a little warmth and bit of rain?" said the King, now rather irritated that all his uneasiness might have been caused by the possibility of no more than a mere thunderstorm or two. "Heavens man, I know we had some flooding in the Autumn and that the Spring this year seems somewhat askew, but surely you are not suggesting that this amounts to one of your Calamities and Things to Worry About?"

"Well Sir," said the Advisor, "there was a time when we all thought this was just as you have described it. Just some oddity in the weather. But..." and here he, too, took a drink from his glass, "but it seems, Sir, we were wrong."

"Wrong!" exclaimed the King, "Do you think I appoint people like you and the Men in White Coats that Know Everything to be wrong?"

"Well, you see, Sir," said the Advisor, now wishing he had not agreed to take on the task of reporting to the King, "there was a time when we, that is when the Men in White Coats, thought that the changes in our weather could just be kept within the limit of what they used to call Plus Two, but now," and he stopped, once more to drink from his glass, spilling a little of the water on the floor, "but now, well now we know it will be, shall we say, somewhat worse than this. In fact, Sir, it could be, well it could be much worse. Some people, some of the men in White Coats that Know Everything, are now talking about what they call Plus Six."

The King was now listening with complete attention. His face was pale and his throat was dry. He could not move or speak. It was as if he had taken a thudding blow to his chest. He was not as ill-informed as he sometimes pretended to be. He had heard of this Plus Six, and he knew it was not at all good.

Not much more was said that day. The Senior Advisor departed leaving the King sitting in silence, his face set in a grim stare and his eyes fixed upon the thick book that the Advisor had left behind. He knew what he had to do. And he was not looking forward to it.

Early the next day, before anyone else had woken, the King went out of his castle by a side door and set off for the forest beyond the castle grounds, following a path he had taken before. He was going to see the Old Woman who lived in a small and rather dark cottage in the middle of the forest. He was not looking forward to seeing her, but he knew he must.

He knew the path well and walked with his head down, not looking to the right or the left, deep in thought and with a growing sense of foreboding. He entered the forest and the path narrowed, twisting and turning its way to the middle. There he stopped. In front of him was the cottage of the Old Woman. Only a thin and turning spiral of smoke rising from the chimney suggested she was at home.

Reluctantly, the King walked up to the cottage door and knocked. No reply. He knocked again, and then saw the Old Woman, dressed in what appeared to be a tattered eiderdown, coming towards him from the back of the cottage carrying a large bucket of water.

"Well are you going to help me carry this bucket or not?" she said in a voice that was both ancient and sharp. "Could you for once in your stupid life not just stand about looking regal, but do something useful – like helping me carry this bucket? I am only carrying it because I knew you would come and see me, and would need some tea; although I may not be able to find my kettle and I doubt I can tell you anything that will help you."

With that the Old Woman dropped the bucket to the ground, the water splashing onto what might have been shoes, but looked more like the husks of some kind of spiky animal.

The King hurried forward, taking up the bucket. It was surprisingly heavy, as if the water in it had come from somewhere deep in the ground. Carrying the bucket with both hands, he followed the Old Woman into her cottage, bending to pass through the low doorway. The room was as he remembered it, dark and with an earthen floor and an open fire, and with furniture covered with jars, tins, piles of old leaves and fruits, and with not just one but several cats draped asleep on shelves and sofas. One twitched an ear and opened an eye as the King came in.

"Put the bucket in the kitchen," commanded the Old Woman, "whilst I see if I can find a kettle." And with that she disappeared into a large cupboard from which came the sound of pots and pans being thrown this way and that, some of them falling to the ground with a great clatter. Eventually, the Old Woman reappeared clutching a large kettle covered with cobwebs. It had obviously not been used for a long time.

"I haven't used this kettle since you were last here with another one of your pitiful questions," said the Old Woman taking off the lid and waiting for the King to pour in some water. This done, the kettle was hung over the open fire to boil, whilst the Old Woman went off in search of a tin of tea, which she found tucked away under a pile of rags beside the sink.

"Now," said the Old Woman, "why don't we just sit down so that you can tell me all about the weather. I assume that is what you have come for?" And with that she pushed one of the cats off the sofa and offered the seat to the King, whilst she sat upon a rocking chair beside the fire, setting it to rock slowly to and fro.

"Well," said the King, dreading what the Old Woman might say to him, "the Men in White Coats…"

But before he could continue, the Old Woman interrupted him.

"Good grief," she said, increasing the rocking of her chair, "don't tell me that these dullards have at last woken up to what anyone with half a brain could have seen ages ago! Don't tell me they have actually come to see what was staring them in the face."

"Well," continued the King, "it would seem that they have."

"Seem?" said the Old Woman, now rocking at a great pace, "What do you mean 'seem'. They either have or they haven't. Which is it?"

"Well," said the King, somewhat flustered and alarmed at the rocking of the Old Woman's chair, "they have now seen that some while ago and for reasons that no-one quite knows, well, that some while ago, we took a wrong turning."

"Wrong turning?" exclaimed the Old Woman with

a crackling laugh. "Is that what they call it? Wrong turning, wrong turning!" And she leapt out of the rocking chair and disappeared into the kitchen, from which there was again a great deal of clattering of china until she returned with a tray upon which was a large cream and crazed teapot and two mugs. She took the kettle from the fire and poured the hot water into the teapot. Then, having let it settle for a minute or two, she poured the tea into the two mugs, taking the large one for herself, and giving the smaller one to the King. She was still chuckling to herself and repeating again and again the words, "wrong turning, wrong turning."

Once the mugs were filled with tea, or what might have been some brew of dubious and unknown provenance, the Old Woman climbed back into her rocking chair. But this time she stopped its rocking and leaning forward looked straight into the eyes of the King.

"Now listen to me," she said, "I shall say this once and only once, since I am tired of giving you advice that you ignore."

The King, too, sat forward and listened.

"You and your people have so disrupted this world with your selfishness, your hatred and your greed that what you call 'the weather' will never again be settled. Not in your lifetime, not in your children's lifetime, not in your grandchildren's lifetime and not in the lifetime of your grandchildren's grandchildren. Do you understand this?"

The King nodded his head, but said nothing.

"There will be dreadful storms of wind and rain, and the seas will rise to a great height. Many of you will not survive. Do you understand this?"

Again, the King nodded his head and said nothing.

"Now," said the Old Woman, "there is only one thing you can do. Are you listening?"

"Yes," said the King. But what he heard took him by surprise.

"The only thing for you to do," said the Old Woman, "is to care for each other and to care for the Earth as if she was your Mother. Tenderness, kindliness and care. These are the qualities that you will need both to limit as much as you can the catastrophe that will come, and then to look after each other when the storms have swept many of you away."

She paused for a moment and set her eyes so deeply upon the King that he felt himself sinking into a deep and dark place, a place that at one and the same time both took away his breath and made him feel as if he had come home.

"I know," said the Old Woman, "that your Men in White Coats, your Bankers and your Advisors will tell you this is nonsense and that all will be well with a slight change to business as usual, but then it was their advice that brought us to where we are; and you must remember that they can no longer hear the voice of the Earth. It's up to you."

And with that, the Old Woman got up from he chair, picked up the tray with the teapot and mugs, and disappeared into her kitchen, leaving the King staring into her fire.

The ending of this story is for you to decide upon. Do you think that the King took the advice of the Old Woman or do you think that he just kept silent and let the Men in White Coats, the Bankers and the Advisors do as they wished? Do you think the storms and the rain came? Do you think the seas rose to a great height? Or do you think these were just the ramblings of an Old Woman who couldn't find her kettle? Do you think the people of the King's realm learnt the lessons of love and a care for each other and the Earth or do you think they, too, thought this was mere nonsense and just went on as usual?

And, of course, what did you do?

FINDING ELSEWHERE

THE STORY OF DREAD

In the land of Dread everything was ruled by fear, and everyone who lived there was fearful. From the moment they woke until the moment they returned to their beds to sleep, the people of Dread were shrouded by fear, and it made them pale and fat. You might suppose that because their lives were so anxious and dreadful they would have been pale and thin, but this was not so. They were pale and fat. Ever seeking comfort, the people of Dread ate and drank as much as they could. From morning to night they ate anything they could find that was sweet and filling – pastries, cereals, burgers and all kinds of chocolate bars, washed down with colas and fizzy fruit-flavoured drinks. And so they were pale and fat.

Two of the main businesses of the land of Dread were factories that produced the foods and drinks consumed by its people, each one advertising its products with pictures of happy people running and jumping about outside in the sunshine and either eating the pastries, cereals, burgers and all kinds of chocolate bars or drinking the colas and fizzy fruit-flavoured drinks.

"How happy and carefree these people are," said the citizens of Dread, "and if I eat this food or drink this drink, then I, too, will be happy and carefree."

But they were not. Nor were they meant to be.

The people who owned the factories of Dread had long ago worked out that whilst their foods and drinks should offer happiness and satisfaction, it was most important that they should never deliver it. It was absolutely necessary that the foods and the drinks should leave the people of Dread feeling unhappy and dissatisfied, so that they would always want to eat and drink even more. Otherwise how would the factory owners achieve their plans to sell more and yet more? Once the people had eaten and drunk, and once they had experienced a short moment of delight, it was absolutely essential that they should, once more, feel anxious, hungry and thirsty. So the factory owners made sure that their products were constantly presented in a different guise or circumstance: different wrappers, different flavours and of course 'two for the price of one'. And so, round and round it went – year after year, youngsters became grown-ups and grown-ups became elderly – generation after generation, each one becoming fatter and paler than the last.

You might have thought that the people of Dread would have come to realise that this circle of fear, and then eating and drinking, and then more fear, and then more eating and drinking, was bound to be very bad for them. But not only were they bombarded by the pictures of the happy and carefree people, they had also become so used to being fearful that they no longer knew there was any other way to be.

Years and years ago, the rulers of Dread, had discovered the power of fear, and it was now so deep within them that no one questioned it. Most especially, they had discovered how important it was that the people of Dread should hear the right kind of stories – stories that showed how fearful the world was, and how it was naturally governed by hatred and violence. Although, of course, most jungles survive by being considerate and co-operative, the stories told in Dread were otherwise. "It's a jungle out there," said the stories, meaning that 'out there' it was brutish and frightening. In fact the rulers of Dread had always made sure the stories that were told showed the people that they were born rotten and bad and that unless they obeyed the rules of Dread they would surely be punished and, when they died, they would go to a realm of pain and fire. And having been told this over and over again, the people of Dread believed it must be so.

In the land of Dread everything was governed by these stories so that the people just assumed them to be true. They had long since learnt to understand that to avoid being hungry they must not only feed themselves now, but have more food than was needed in case they felt hungry later. And so, year after year and age after age, they had produced more than they needed. And as they had done this, their population had grown and grown and grown.

The trouble was their story was self-fulfilling, for

as they grew and grew, so they did indeed need to consume more and more. And as they produced more and more, so indeed they grew and grew. It was hardly surprising that they had become by far and away the fattest and most dominant species on Earth. And so it remained, only more so.

Many years ago, the whole economy of Dread had become shaped by this fear of never having enough and so always producing more and more. At first it was food and drink, but then it became just about anything that could be produced and for which a need could be manufactured – more pots and pans, more shoes and trousers, more horses and carts and, in time, more cars and aeroplanes, more televisions, freezers and all kinds of electronic devices. But the more they had, the more it seemed that there was never enough, and as more and more was produced, so it was that the population of Dread grew and grew and grew, the boundaries of Dread being pushed out further and further, destroying anything that got in the way.

As the realm of Dread spread wider and wider, the rulers of Dread came to understand that in order to keep safe all that they had, and in order to have enough of everything they needed, they had to have an army to protect them. In turn, these armies also grew and grew, and as they did so, they needed to have more and more weapons. And the more weapons they had, the more enemies they seemed to have, so that, as the threats increased, new weapons had to be produced that were even more effective than the ones before. And before long many new factories were built for the making and selling of the weapons of war. In fact, these businesses soon came to be one of the biggest forms of enterprise in Dread, growing larger and larger and employing more and more people, as more and more stories were told of fearful dangers and fearful enemies, none of whom, as it happens, the people of Dread had ever met.

Alongside all of this growth in enterprise grew the need for more and more money, which had to be managed by more and more banks, who themselves grew to be larger and larger until they were so large that they became wondrously powerful. And because what they did was so difficult to understand, they had to pay themselves larger and larger salaries and bonuses, which made them rich beyond the wildest dreams of most of the people of Dread. Indeed, they soon became so wondrously powerful and clever that when they made a mistake, such as losing very large sums of other people's money, it was agreed by the rulers of Dread that everyone else – everyone who was much poorer than they were – should help them out by giving them even more of their money to play with.

Eventually it was understood by the factory owners, by the arms manufacturers, by the bankers and by the rulers of Dread, that the most important thing to do was to grow without limit. Everything had to grow. Because the economy had to grow, consumption had to grow; and because wages had, of course, to be held back to maintain profitability, borrowing had to grow so that the people could continue to spend more. This meant that the bankers had to create more and more money by increasing credit and loans, which, of course, meant that more and more people of Dread found themselves in debt.

You might have supposed that this was rather a

risky thing to do, but because the stories of Dread had made it clear that progress and improvement were always necessary, and that progress and improvement depended upon a growing economy and what was known as 'the trickle down effect', no one for a moment questioned it – although it seemed that the trickle down was not nearly as effective as the trickle up. Nevertheless, it was apparently self-evident that everything had to grow. More and more was always needed, and there was never enough of anything.

HOWEVER...

Largely unknown to the people of Dread, as their consumption of everything was growing, much was being lost. The list of things lost or in danger of being lost included: bees, hares, mayflies, turtledoves, sparrows, wagtails, partridges, heron gulls, hedgehogs, butterflies, toads, bumblebees, moths, beetles and other insects, stocks of fish in the sea, levels and the quality of topsoil, and sources of fresh drinking water.

At the same time, there were growing signs of dis-ease. As the people of Dread grew fatter, there were increasing numbers of suicides, and increasing numbers of people were suffering from stress, anxiety and depression. Increasing numbers had unmanageable levels of debt, and there was a widening gap between the rich and the poor and, indeed, a widening gap between the very rich and everyone else. There was an increase in the numbers of innocent women and children killed by war in distant places and an increase in the number and severity of devastating rainstorms and flooding.

But the people of Dread did not know about these things. They were too busy trying to cope with their own fear, fearful as to whether they would have enough of all the things they were told they needed, fearful of whether they could afford to repay their loans, and thoughtless of what this might mean for anyone but themselves. And this was how they were meant to be, for the stories they had been told did not allow for the possibility that they might be wrong in assuming that there must always be more and more or that it was possible that their wellbeing was entangled with the wellbeing of other people and with the wellbeing of the Earth.

You might think this could not go on, but it did, because the stories of Dread were founded upon ignorance and delusion. The sages have always known that ignorance and delusion give rise to suffering. That is just the way it is. No one in Dread knew this, but that is the way it is. And blind ignorance and blind delusion are especially likely to bring about catastrophic suffering – in time.

So, when the Great Storms came, no one was prepared. There had been some talk of unusual patterns of weather, but it was expected that these would be few and far between. No one had expected the storms to merge together and to grow together. And when it happened, it happened so quickly that there was no time to send out warnings.

The people of Dread had always been told that it was distant, poor people that would suffer. The melting of the ice caps had 'displaced' tens of millions, and unusual droughts and then flooding had 'displaced' many more, but they were always far away. Changes in sea temperature had sometimes held storms in one place, increasing seasonal rainfalls, but the coming together of such a large number of storms all at the same time, one building upon the other and covering the whole of Dread … that had not been expected.

And so, when the Great Storms came, everyone suffered – rich and poor alike, those close by and those far away. And the suffering was very great.

Before then, the rulers of Dread had been advised that the highest wind scale imaginable was winds of 160 miles per hour, or perhaps a little more. No one had foreseen winds in excess of 300 miles per hour. And no one had foreseen what this would do to the height of the waves. There had been talk of waves of 75 feet in exceptional circumstances, but not of waves of more than 150 feet – waves that, when they came, destroyed large parts of the coastal cities of Dread, driving up the rivers with terrifying speed and ferocity, sweeping all before them. That night, many millions of the people of Dread were drowned.

Of course the flooding was everywhere, and with power stations quickly overwhelmed, the lights went out. With roads and railways devastated and closed, those supermarkets that were still standing ran out of food after a few days. And because the flooding damaged the drains and sewerage systems, supplies of clean water soon became inadequate. Within a month or two the people of Dread had huddled together in small 'tribal' groups to defend what they had. There were many skirmishes and some killing too.

None of the government's disaster plans could be put into effect as the devastation had been so much greater than supposed, and in any event the rulers of Dread and their advisors – factory owners and bankers, many of whom lived in large houses close to the coast and the rivers – had been all but swept away. The financial system, of course, collapsed: no electric grid, no power; no power, no telecommunications; no telecommunications, no banking; no banking, no banks; no banks, no money.

Those who survived the trauma of the Great Storms had to find some way of carrying on, of protecting their small communities in the countryside, and transforming urban areas by finding any place they could to grow food. They searched for those places where the water was uncontaminated or built irrigation systems for the vegetable gardens that began to appear throughout the city areas. For a while, and in some places, makeshift armies of soldiers patrolled the streets trying to bring back some sense of order, but it was a wretched task. Some looters were shot, but others came back because for many it was their only way to survive – they took food if they could find it, tools, medicines and any wood or other building materials. It was not long before most of the soldiers just walked away and went off in search of their families.

Now, so many years later, those dreadful times are still held deep within the memories of the people of Dread, and their children listen to stories of a world they cannot recognise, a world of cars and computers, of television and fizzy drinks – and the coming of the Great Storms.

After the first year or two of chaos, a new order began to emerge. Gathered together in their new tribes, the people of Dread began to recover, slowly. To begin with, all of their time was taken in making a safe place to live, with food, water and shelter. And of course burying the dead, although some of the city areas were just abandoned, attracting crows and rats and foxes, whose numbers grew and grew on the easy pickings of carrion. And flies everywhere, large blue and black flies. No one but the looters went to these parts of Dread and anyway, after the first week or two, there was nothing useful left to take.

Life was best in the countryside, in villages surrounded by barricades. At first, living in fear, people were very defensive and hostile to outsiders. But then, the men and women of the villages discovered they had relatives and friends in other villages close by and they wanted to meet up and talk to them, to see how they were coping and to share their experiences of trying to provide for their families. And so, as it became apparent that they needed to become more trusting of each other, they found ways of co-operating. New relationships and a regular gathering together began to emerge.

Because of all that has happened, new stories are now being told – stories of families and of hardship, stories of solace and a caring for each other. Somehow, the people of Dread know that they cannot return to the old ways, the ways before the Great Storms. And as their fear has eased, they have talked more and more about how they might live in accordance with the laws of the Earth; how to live in ways that sustain the lives and the health of their families; how to care for their parents and neighbours; how to survive with local materials and seeds; how to have enough without taking too much. This is what they are talking about now. And as they do so, new towns are beginning to be built, bringing together some of the villages into a new and shared community.

People don't travel far from home, but they have begun to trade with each other, using what is left of the roads and pathways. In some places it is possible to move about more easily than in others, especially where the storms did not destroy stables and horses. Old carts have been pulled out of museums and, working together, people have soon rediscovered the skills needed to make wheels and new carts. Blacksmiths are much in demand and attract a good many young apprentices. Building skills and those of farming and horticulture are what are wanted, as are those of doctors and nurses who can work without using the old drugs and equipment, which were destroyed the Great Storms. And within each area there are projects to repair hospitals, where possible restoring equipment and operating theatres.

Of course, finding ways to create energy to 'power up' was a struggle at first, but some power stations and grids had survived, and before long groups of people came together to find ways of utilising wind and solar in better ways. In fact, the people of Dread discovered that ways of utilising these forms of energy had already been well developed in the old days of Dread, but had been held back by their rulers and by the owners of the old power stations and power grids. Now, many men and women have come forward with knowledge of what to do and they have been welcomed and given every support.

Because it soon became obvious that people would have to share their houses to provide shelter for those who had nowhere else to go, the old ways of ownership have declined. Many have agreed that their houses should be held in common in small communities, as this makes it easier for people to find a place to live without becoming burdened by debt. Out of sheer necessity, the sharing of land and water by common governance has now become widely spread, and, if anything, people are relieved to live in community. They no longer have any interest in 'rising house prices'.

Some parts remain deserted, now overgrown by briars and scrub. One day, perhaps one day, people will inhabit them again, but for now no one goes there. Other parts remain hostile and fractured, but more and more of the people of Dread seem to be finding something worthwhile, something that works for them and their families and communities. This is not where they wanted to be. It is still a difficult place with its own sorrow. But it is a beginning.

Remember this. For we are the people of Dread.

FINDING ELSEWHERE

THE TWO BROTHERS

Once upon a time there were two brothers. Together, they farmed the fields and the hills that had belonged to their family for many generations. One of them was a herdsman, looking after his cows and sheep. The other was a farmer, looking after a smallholding on which he grew corn and vegetables. For many years the two brothers lived happily side by side. The muck from the animals was used to fertilise the farmer's fields and the corn of the farmer was used to feed the cows of the herdsman.

Then one day the farmer spoke to his brother and said, "Brother, the land that you are using for grazing is too good for your animals. Why don't I take it over and you move further away where the land is less good, but fit for cows and sheep. Then I will be able to grow more corn for your stock?"

And so the brothers agreed to do this and for some while they lived happily side by side. Then one day the farmer spoke to his brother again and said, "Brother, it makes no sense for you to graze your cows in one place and then bring them to me for corn. Wouldn't it be better if I took over your herd and the pastures on which they graze and you moved further up the hill with your sheep? Then I could let you have some of the milk and you would be free to look after your sheep?"

And so the brothers agreed to do this and for some while they lived happily side by side, although now that the land of the farmer had spread so far and his brother had to spend all his time in the distant hills, they hardly ever spoke to each other. Soon, the farmer stopped providing milk for his brother, but sold it in the nearby town. Life on the hill became harder and harder and some years later, on one particularly cold Winter's night, the brother who was looking after what was left of his flock of sheep died. When his body was discovered some days later, it was buried on the hill and his brother, the farmer, took over the hillside, so that he now owned all the family's land.

Having no use for the hillside and no knowledge of how to look after sheep, the farmer left the sheep there and forgot about them. Some while later a pack of wolves came hunting for food and devoured what remained of the sheep. Then, encouraged by this find, they looked down the hill at the cows grazing on the pasture. Over the next few months, one by one and sometimes two at a time, the cows were killed and eaten by the wolves, whose pack was becoming stronger and stronger. It was not long before the farmer had lost all of his cows.

And then one day there was a terrible storm, with

thunder, lightning and a deluge of rain. The streams of the hillside were in full flood and ran down and into the river in the valley where the farmer lived. The river was soon more swollen than it had ever been and before long it was overflowing onto the farmer's land, destroying his crops and washing away his fences. Then, the clouds burst apart and a torrent of rain fell upon the valley sweeping away the farmer's house and all his possessions. For a while the farmer clung onto a floating log, but then he too was gone.

Sheltering behind some rocks on the hillside, the pack of wolves looked down into the valley and wondered where they would go to next.

FINDING ELSEWHERE

THE KING WHO LOST HIS MEMORY

O nce upon a time there lived a King and the King had grown old and sad. One night, one cold Winter's night, he dreamed a fearful dream. An Old Woman entered his chamber. She was wearing a dark cloak with a hood, but deep within the folds of the hood the King thought he could see a dreadful face, the skin marked by warts and the lips twisted and thick.

"Who are you, who are you!" cried the King. "Why are you here and what do you want from me?"

"You fool," hissed the Old Woman. "You great fool. You deserve nothing but shame. You do not remember my name and yet you ask me what I want from you. Do you really believe that you have anything to give me? You are useless to me. You have let your land go to waste, the soil is like dust and the waters are foul". And uttering a fearful shriek the Old Woman threw back her hood to reveal the ugliest and the most grotesque face that the King had ever seen, a face with a nose like the snout of a pig and...

"No, no, no!" cried the King and he leapt from his bed, pulling the sheets around him, his eyes now wide open and staring into the darkness, his whole body trembling.

All was quiet... and the King sat there, on the floor in the middle of his chamber, until at last and to his great relief he could see the first pink traces of dawn feeling their way across the sky.

Wrapping himself in his sheets, he climbed the staircase that led from his chamber to a tower set high in his castle from where he could see, all around him, his city and the furthest parts of his realm. And as he looked, tears came to his eyes, for he knew that his city, which had once been bright like the sun, was now dull and ugly, and the countryside, which once had been green and fertile, was now barren and dying. But he could not remember how it had happened. Nor could he remember what it was that he should do to restore the land. The King was frightened.

He hurried back to his chamber and sent at once for the wisest of his wise men – the Minister of Ways and Means and the Minister of Whys and Wherefores.

"Surely," he said to himself, "these men who know the ways of the world – who know how things are and why they must be – surely they will be able to help me?"

Each one came and each one went. Each spoke at length, and in a high tone and a forceful manner. But nothing that they said was of any help to the King.

No help at all.

Shaken and now even more frightened than before, the King asked to be left alone, quite alone. Indeed, he remained alone not just for the rest of that day but for the rest of that week... and the next week too. Day after day, he sat at the table before the window of his chamber not knowing what to do. And the more he sat, the more his sadness grew.

And then, one morning as he stared out of his window, he saw a thin column of smoke rising in a spiral above a grove of trees that stood beyond the walls of the city. He called for his Page, who entered the chamber somewhat nervously.

"What," enquired the King, "is that column of smoke that I see beyond the walls of the city?"

The Page looked out of the window. "That smoke," he said, " that smoke is the smoke of a fire."

The King turned his tired eyes to look upon the anxious face of the Page. "I know that the smoke is the smoke of a fire," said the King somewhat shortly, "but what fire does it come from?"

The Page once more looked out of the window. "That smoke," he replied, "that smoke is the smoke of the fire of the hut of the wise and aged Hermit."

"And what," said the King, "is the name of the Hermit?"

"The name of the Hermit," said the Page, hoping that the interrogation would now come to an end, "the name of the Hermit is Bramble McGregor Smith, but everyone calls him Old Man."

At once, the King knew that it was to the Hermit that he must speak, and he sent the Page to bring him to his chamber.

And the Hermit came to the King and the King told him all that he had heard and seen, both in the dream and from the tower of his castle.

"Thus," said the King, "I fear that the worries of state and of commerce have distracted me so that I have failed to protect my realm. My Ministers can say nothing that will help me. And what is worse, I have lost my memory and do not know what it is that I must do to restore the land."

"My dearest King," said the Hermit, wrapping his capacious robe around himself and biting on his thumb, "it is true that you have been distracted by the worries of state and of commerce, and that your city, your fields and your woods are dying. And it is true that your Ministers cannot help you. I say nothing about your dream, but if you really wish to restore your land, you must make a journey with me, and you must make it as soon as possible."

The King held forth his hand and asked that the journey be made at once.

"So be it," said the Hermit. "Come to me this evening, and bring with you the woven bag that you will find within the blanket box beneath your bed." And with that he departed.

Once the Hermit had gone, the King pulled the blanket box from beneath his bed and, much to his surprise, found within it a beautiful bag, woven of many colours – red and yellow, green and gold.

All day long he prepared himself, and in the evening he walked out from the city to meet the

Hermit, taking his bag with him.

The King followed the path towards the grove of trees and soon saw before him the Hermit's hut, the open door letting in the last rays of the setting sun. But now, with each step, the King felt, at first uneasy, and then afraid. The air was chill and there was a strange and foreboding silence. The King looked around and everything was still, not a breeze, not a sound.

He knocked on the door but there was no reply.

"Are you there, Old Man?" called the King.

No sound.

"It is me, the King."

Not a word.

"Perhaps I should not have come," thought the King to himself, and was about to turn away when a voice from within the hut called, "Come on in, I am here."

The King pushed open the door and peered into the faint light of the hut. He could see nothing but as his eyes adjusted to the darkness he saw, at first, and lying discarded in a bundle on the floor, the Hermit's robe, and then…

Sitting upright before the fireplace was not the Hermit but a large grey Wolf, who stared directly at the King with what appeared to be a look of considerable satisfaction.

"Do come in," said the Wolf, fixing the King with eyes that were dark and deep and with a broad smile that showed, behind soft grey lip a set of the whitest teeth that you will ever have seen. "I have supper ready for you." And with that the Wolf placed before the King a bowl of soup, a plate of bread and a goblet of wine.

"Where," said the King, struggling to remain calm, "is the Old Man?"

"Ah!" replied the Wolf, "I am afraid that he had to go away."

"But," said the King, his heart beating like a hammer in his chest, "he had agreed to take me on a journey to help me regain my memory and restore my land."

"Yes," said the Wolf, tilting his head to one side as if he had just remembered something delicious, "he told me of this before… before he went away. And since I am here, and since, at the moment, I have nothing better to do, I will be your guide. Now you really must have your supper."

So the King sat down and began to eat, and as he ate the Wolf spoke to him.

"The path that we shall take," said the Wolf, now getting up and walking in a circle around the table at which the King sat, "follows the path of the sun and the moon. It turns in the form of a spiral, drawing whoever will follow beyond the realm of the present into the realm of memory and imagination.

"We shall turn sun-wise, from sunrise to sunset, through Winter, Spring, Summer and Autumn, through the Four Directions, the Four Elements, the Four Ages and the Four Seasons. We shall follow the path of our ancestors, moon-wise through the sacred festivals of the year. For the year is divided into two parts – the dark half, which runs from Samhain to Beltane, from November to April, and the Light Half, which runs from Beltane to Samhain, from May to October. The festival of Imbolc divides the dark half of the year into Winter and Spring, and the festival of Lugnasadh divides the light half into Summer and Autumn.

"And in the Centre of the Wheel of the Year stands the Tree of Life, stretching Above and Below into the Otherworlds – linking the Middle World with the Upper World of knowledge and inspiration and the Lower World of our ancestors, the place of power. The Centre and the Eight Directions form a Sacred Circle of Nine. And as we make our journey, and as you recover your memory, you will gather the gifts of the Year and place them in your woven bag, which I see is of many colours. All this you must know both in your head and in your heart. Rest here tonight and then…"

Warmed by his supper, and entranced by the slow circling of the Wolf, the King fell into a deep sleep.

It was the time before dawn and the Wolf and the King stood at the edge of the grove of trees, facing the North-East. The Wolf stretched himself and spoke.

"The Eight Directions will mark our journey, turning with the sun and the moon. But now, before we start, stand and look towards the horizon. With arms outstretched acknowledge where you stand – before and behind, around to one side and then to the other, let your arms follow your fingertips as you turn."

And so the King turned, trying, nevertheless, to keep one eye on the Wolf.

"And now," said the Wolf, "raise your head to the sky above, not just to the canopy of the sky but to the great heights of the Cosmos. Feel the ground below your feet, not just the surface of the ground but the great depths of the Earth."

And the King did so.

The Wolf continued, his voice even and clear. "This is the time before the Beginning, the time of preparation, the time of initiation. In the Great Calendar of the year it is the time of the snowdrop, the first signs of growth after the healing darkness of Winter. Now, O King, do you remember this time?"

There was silence, and for a while the face of the King looked sad as he tried to find his memory. Some minutes passed before the King spoke.

"I think," said the King, "I think…" But he could recall nothing.

"It's no good just thinking," said the Wolf. "You won't regain your memory by thinking. Feel the earth begin to awaken. See how Venus, the Morning Star, welcomes the dawn. Listen to the cry of the newborn lambs. After the long wait of the Winter, there is now fresh milk and meat. This is the first day of Spring. At last we begin to sense the possibility of renewal, not yet manifest but soon to come. Winter still marks the land, but we have left behind the Darkest Depths and aconites and daffodils stand as a first reminder of all that is to come. There are catkins, and soon the hedges will begin to break and the almond tree will be in blossom. This is the time that is called the Cleansing Tide, the time when the land is washed clean by snow and the rain. It is the time of Candlemas.

"And what is more," said the Wolf, turning now to look directly at the King, "it is the festival of Imbolc. It is the time of Brigit, keeper of fire, goddess of wisdom and of the poets, mother of memory. She is the Cailleach transformed into the Maiden. She is St Brigit, foster-mother of Christ, bringing the new milk at lambing time. She is the goddess of healing and childbirth. Ask, now for the gift of the North-East."

And so, in the stillness of dawn, the King stood quietly, letting go... And he asked Brigit for her gift and when he received it he placed it in his bag, the woven bag of many colours.

"We must go now," said the Wolf. "Follow me, for we must meet the sunrise."

And so, together, they set off, along the path of the sun until they came to a small chapel. They followed the path around the chapel until they stood at its eastern end. Here the Wolf stopped and drawing the King to his side, ordered him to take off his socks and shoes.

The King, who now seemed to have forgotten that he was talking to a Wolf, did so.

"We stand to face the rising sun, O King. Before us, in the East, rays of light have already begun to colour the sky. This is a time of Beginning."

The sun had begun to rise, but the wind still carried the chill of the night. Standing barefoot, the King could now feel the ground, wet with dew beneath his feet. He could see the sun appearing above the horizon and could hear the birds singing their morning song. Again, the Wolf spoke.

"Feel once again the renewal of the Earth. Your feet connect you with the land, they are your foothold, your foundation. To be at one with the land, you need to stand in this way upon the ground. This is the time of Innocence. Do you remember this time, O King?"

Again there was silence, but then, rather hesitantly, the King began to speak.

"I do remember. I do sort of remember this time," he said, "for as the sun rises we begin to feel its warmth. I remember that this is the season of planting. The horse chestnut tree is opening its buds and the primroses are in flower. I remember..."

But then it was gone and the cloud of forgetfulness had returned.

"Never mind," said the Wolf, "the path has begun."

And he walked sun-wise, in a circle around the King.

"Follow me, for this is the time of Easter, of resurrection and of rebirth. This is the time when the seed is sown and when prayers are said for the fertility of the soil. It is also the time of the Spring Equinox, the time when the days and the nights are of equal length, the time of the magical Hare, and of Eostra the goddess of the Dawn of the Year. The hot crossed buns of Good Friday, which celebrate the Resurrection of Christ, also bear the mark of the Four Directions, representing the Wheel of the Year."

"So be it," said the King and they stood in prayer.

In the East it is the morning,
The Breath of life.
Hear our prayer.

"Listen well, O King," said the Wolf. "The East is a good place to start from, for the East brings us light, it is the place for finding our way and purpose. It is the path of the child with eyes of wonder. We cannot begin our journey until we have a sense of direction, and how shall we find our way if we do not know and cannot express the dimensions and order of space? But our journey is only just beginning and we must now quicken our pace. We journey to regain your memory and to restore your land. Stand now and ask the East for her gift."

And the King did so and placed the gift carefully into his bag, the woven bag of many colours.

"Follow me, follow me," commanded the Wolf, spinning on his paws and setting off in the direction of the sun. And the King turned, shoes and socks in hand, and ran off after the Wolf.

"We turn to the South-East," called out the Wolf without bothering to turn his head to see if the King could hear him. "We are on our way to the festival of Beltane, the threshold between Spring and Summer. If this does not cheer you up nothing will. For Beltane marks the end of the dark half of the year and the start of the light. I am sure that we shall begin to find your memory here."

And they strode on and on until they turned a corner in the pathway and found themselves following a gentle slope down towards the outer edges of a small town. Beside the path were banks of sheep's parsley and white roses, and the first of the swallows sweeping through the air. Before them they could see a field and a throng of people dancing with coloured ribbons around a May Pole.

The King stood and looked towards the town. Again his memory stirred and now he began to recognise the splendour of the early summer's day. He saw coming towards him a beautiful young woman, her hair plaited with flowers and her dress embroidered with columbine and roses pink and yellow. She came up to the King and, with a smile, held out her hand to him. Unsure of himself, at first he hesitated. But then he moved forward to take her hand... and she was gone and all that he could see was the dance of the May Pole. The shock struck the King like a bolt of lightning!

"Do you remember this, O King?" cried the Wolf.

"I do," replied the King, as the vision of the flower-maiden and memories of his youth rushed through his body. "I do remember. This is May Day, the time of the May Queen, the day that we celebrate the fertility of the land. In the hedgerow, the may is in flower and I can feel the warmth of Summer. 'Cast not a clout 'til May be out,'" he cried, now feeling quite comfortable with the Wolf's company.

"Naturally not," said the Wolf, smiling to see how the spirits of the King were awakened. "Remember this time well, O King, and feel the energy begin to grow within you as it does within the land. But tread with care. For the gates between this world and the Otherworld are ajar and the spirits of the land are abroad. Take care lest they entrance you and try to take you with them to the faery realm." And he danced a few steps around the May Pole, holding one of the ribbons gently in his mouth.

The King, too, could feel the power of the land growing within him but, remembering his instructions, he stood still with the palms of his hands uplifted and asked the White Lady for her gift, placing it into his bag, the woven bag of many colours.

"Come on," called the Wolf, and the King looked up to see that his companion had already set off along the path of the sun as it rose higher and higher in the sky, taking them into the centre of the town. By the time the King had caught up with him, the Wolf was standing in the market place, drinking from the fountain. It was noontide and, although no one seemed to notice them, all around the King could hear the sounds of the day, the restless sounds of work and of the hustle and bustle of people coming and going. The sun stood high above them and the ground beneath their feet was hot and dry.

"The bright light of the South is on your face," said the Wolf. "This is the time of power and energy, it is the time of growth and of ripening. It is the time of coming into being, the time of Fire and courage. This is the place of the strong and the brave, those that welcome knowledge and learn fast. Do not seek the shade, for this is the time of commitment. If you are to sustain your memory and restore your land, you will need the life-giving, life-bearing, energy, fertility and strength of your body – you will need your belly, your 'guts'."

In the South it is noontide,
The energy of Fire.
Hear our prayer.

"It is Midsummer's Day, the Summer Solstice, the longest day of the year. Do you remember such a time, O King?"

"I do," said the King, his memory now returning to him with ever increasing strength, "and on St John's Eve we light bonfires to celebrate the Sun at its zenith. We take torches of flame and circle our fields, marking our boundaries and blessing the land with light, calling upon the Harvest Mother to grant us a good harvest. Summer is a time of pilgrimage, Holy Days and Holy Places marking the way of the traveller. And, at Glastonbury, the resting place of the Grail, my people gather beneath the Tor in the chapel dedicated to Mary the Virgin, Mother of God. The Morris Men dance for the fertility of the earth and it is said that women dance their secret dances of the moon. The gardens are abundant, with white roses in full flower, and the candle-blossom is on the horse chestnut tree. There are new potatoes, summer spinach, Canterbury Pink and Sweet Williams. This is the season of strawberries and of summer pudding."

"Feel the breath of the South Wind as we turn towards it," said the Wolf, "and the ground beneath our feet is warm and fertile. The seed that falls in Autumn, is given life in the dark ground of Winter. It is born in the Spring and now grows in the warm sun of the Summer. Stand, O King, and ask the Summer for her gift – and then we shall have some lunch."

And the King stood, arms upraised, and asked the Summer for her gift, which he placed in his bag, the woven bag of many colours.

After he had done so, the Wolf produced, apparently from nowhere, two egg and salad sandwiches and two bowls of rice, which they ate hungrily for it was the first food that they had eaten that day.

Licking his lips with his long pink tongue, the Wolf collected up the bowls, washing them first in the fountain of the market place.

"Come now," said the Wolf. "Again, the spiral turns." And they set off, leaving the town behind them.

After a while, they found themselves in fields of swaying corn, ripe and ready to be harvested – the First Harvest of the year.

"We face the South-West," said the Wolf, "and this is the time of the festival of Lughnasadh, a time of binding and obligation, a time to recognise our responsibility to the land. It was at this time that the great and glorious Lugh brought honour to his foster-mother Taitlin on the day of her funeral."

"It is the festival of Lammas," said the King, no longer needing to be prompted, "the celebration of the Loaf Mass."

"This is the path that leads to love," said the Wolf, as if he, too, were remembering something from a long time ago. "Ask for your gift, O King."

The King stood, and asked for his gift, and as he did so he saw before him the figure of a woman seated upon the ground and clad in a golden robe embroidered with ears of corn, a crown upon her head. In one hand she carried the rowan-wand of healing, whilst she cradled a child suckling at her breast. The King acknowledged her and placed her gift into his bag, the woven bag of many colours.

They turned together and set out along the path that was leading them across open fields towards the sea into which the sun was falling. They stopped upon a bluff overlooking the sea, looking across the water towards the shadow of a distant island.

"That," said the Wolf, "is the island of the Apple Woman. For we have walked all day from sunrise to sunset and now we stand and face the West. The wind of the West brings us rain and behind us in the East the moon is rising. The sun has left the South and now falls beneath the horizon. The darkness will come from the North."

> In the West it is evening,
> The Waters of reflection,
> Hear our prayer".

"Is this not the time of the Autumnal Equinox, of Michelmas, of St Michael?" asked the King, his memory now clear and fresh.

"It is," said the Wolf, "and some say that St Michael took on the mantle of the Sun God. Many hilltop churches dedicated to him and to St George and St Mary are thought to be aligned with each other along the mysterious ley lines of earth energy. This Line of the Sunrise, runs from St Michael's Mount, in the West, via Glastonbury, Avebury and through sixty churches until it reaches Hopton in Suffolk, in the most eastern part of your realm, O King."

"The First Harvest, the harvest of corn has been

gathered in," said the King, "and now it is time for the harvest of fruit and berries, the harvest of the orchard, the hedgerow and the coppice. The Wheel of the Year turns, the trees begin to change colour, letting go of the greenery of Summer for the deeper shades of Autumn, and the swallows gather in flocks to follow the sun. When they have gone we will close the hayloft door where they have nested. The harvesters have arrived, attracted by the light of the candle and the screech owl is back in the garden. Soon the mice will come back into the house for warmth."

"It is the evening of the day," said the Wolf, "a time for being together, for closing in, a time for family and friends. It is a time of story-telling and of sharing food together." And once more, from nowhere, he produced their food – two bowls of soup and two bread rolls. "This is the path of maturity. Let us sit quietly beneath the trees for this is the place of secret wisdom and of healing, the place of the heart. Attend to this, for unless you have compassion you have no remembrance and you cannot restore your land."

The King sat down, now leaning his back against the reclining form of the Wolf. He ate his supper in silence, letting his eyes drift out across the sea to the mysterious island on the horizon. As he did so, he felt his heart fill with the love for his land and he thanked the goddess of the West for her gift, placing it into his bag, the woven bag of many colours.

The sun had set, and in the dusk the Wolf and the King now walked on together in silence, making their way to the North-West and to the scared grove where the Hermit lived. The stars were bright in the sky and the full moon gave them light. They now walked step for step, sure of the ground beneath their feet, passing by bushes covered with the darkest blackberries that shone in the moonlight.

Eventually they found themselves at the Hermit's hut and the Wolf pushed open the door. The King followed him inside to find him, as before, sitting in silence in front of the open fireplace, the fire already alight and burning with a deep and intense flame. The King took a chair from the table and sat beside him.

"We are at the time of Samhain," said the Wolf, "the festival of Halloween, of All Souls and of Martinmas, the beginning of Winter. Our journey has restored your memory and brought you back to your land."

"I know," said the King, and they sat side by side, staring into the fire. "I have much to thank you for," said the King, now looking with affection into the deep dark eyes of the Wolf. "What can I do to repay you?"

The Wolf looked for a long time at the King, and then he spoke. "At this time of the year, the doors are open between this world and the Otherworld, and the spirits of those that are dead and of those that are yet to be born to walk amongst us."

Once again there was silence, before the Wolf, spoke. "Do you see, O King, the silver-handled knife that lies upon the table?"

"I do," he replied running his thumb along its edge.

"Then," said the Wolf, now standing to his full height, "take up the knife and thrust it into my breast."

The words struck deep into the King, hitting him

in his belly. "No! No!" he cried, "You have been my guide and now you have become my friend."

"Nevertheless," said the Wolf, now once more holding the King with his eyes, "if you would thank me, thrust the blade into my breast."

The King stared at the Wolf, looking deep into his eyes, unable to move. Then he saw, standing behind the Wolf, the figure of the old crone, but now serene and still.

"You have come this far, O King," said the crone. "Your memory is restored and now you must complete your journey. Take my gift." And so saying she took up the knife from the table and placed it into the King's hands.

The King continued to stare into the eyes of the Wolf. No movement, no sound. It was as if time itself had stopped. The King clasped the handle of the knife in both hands, his arms held out straight before him. He lifted his arms above his head and then...

...And then he plunged the knife into the breast of the Wolf. He waited for the Wolf's cry, his eyes closed lest he should see the blood on the knife. There was no cry.

And when at last he opened his eyes, there was no knife... and no Wolf. Only the Hermit, kneeling before the fireplace and prodding the burning wood with a long poker.

"What... how... where..." stumbled the King.

But the Hermit turned to him, placing his finger to his lips. "No questions and no answers," he said.

The King and the Hermit sat together by the hearth in silence.

"Soon I shall leave you," said the Hermit, "but now you must rest, for tomorrow you have much work to do."

"I shall be ready," said the King.

"Remember to ask for the gift of the North, O King, for this is the place of wisdom and transformation."

"I shall remember," said the King.

In the North it is darkness,
The wisdom of the Earth.
Hear our prayer.

And the King slept and the snow fell upon the Earth. That night the Old Woman came again to the King in his dream. But now the King was not afraid and waited quietly for her to remove the hood of her cloak. Now he looked gently upon her face, for there too was the face of the flower-maiden and the face of the Queen and the sound of the water running and leaves falling in Autumn.

"And do you now remember my name?" said the Old Woman.

"You have no name," said the King, "but you are the weaver of dreams and you spin the Wheel of the Year. I am your servant."

The King awoke to find himself sitting on the ground in front of the Hermit's hut amidst the grove of trees, the snowdrops and aconites like white and yellow stars in a carpet of green and brown. He rubbed his eyes and then his head. He stood and stretched, his arms at once turning in a circle that followed his fingertips. He looked around but no one was there.

"This is very strange," he thought to himself. "How did I get here? And why do I have no socks or shoes on my feet? I must have been dreaming."

But then he noticed on the ground a beautiful bag woven of many colours – red and yellow, green and gold. He knelt down and looked into the bag and there they were, the gifts of the Year. Then the King remembered and, picking up the bag, he walked away from the sacred grove towards the city to start his work.

And as he walked he saw that the land was showing the first signs of Spring and that the lambs were suckling the milk of the ewes. His step was light as he walked. From the East came the Breath of life, from the South the energy of Fire, from the West the Waters of reflection, and from the North the wisdom of the Earth.

And in the Centre
Is the Great Tree
Above and Below
And all is one.

Divine Mother, Divine Father, hear our prayer.

And there they were, the gifts of the Year.

FINDING ELSEWHERE

THE GREAT QUEEN AND THE GATEKEEPER'S SON

Once upon a time there was a great Queen and her lands extended as far as the eye could see and beyond: from the green hills of the morning in the East to the shores of the West where the long waves of evening beat upon the sand; in the South her lands were covered with vines, orchards and bee hives and in the North snow-capped mountains rose into the sky and seemed to touch the stars. She had domain over all the land and for its governance and protection she took to her side, as King, a husband – one who had proved himself to be brave in arms and in heart.

For many years the land prospered, giving forth an abundance of apples, pears, grapes and honey. The trees grew strong and the rivers and streams flowed with clear water. All that lived in the land dwelt in peace and harmony. But then, one day, the King fell ill. No one could say why it had happened, but the more his sickness grew the more he withdrew from his people until, in time, he took to his bed and lay there, his face pale and his throat dry.

The wisest of the wise were asked for their advice but to no avail. The King became weaker and weaker and as he did so something strange and shocking occurred. Day by day, as the vitality of life drained from the King's eyes and lips so, too, the land seemed to waste away. First, the rivers lost their full flow of water, in some cases withering to no more than a trickle. Then the vegetable beds in the orchards failed, the trees lost their topmost branches, the vines lost their bloom and the bees abandoned their hives.

The great Queen was overcome with a deep sadness, for she loved the King, had chosen him as guardian of her lands and had guided him in all that he had done. She had been with him when the vines were planted and when the hives were set. She had walked with him through the orchards and fields at harvest time and sat with him beside the rivers and streams. But now the time had come and as the moon waned she, too, left the city and withdrew into the high mountains of the North.

The city and all the land was left in darkness and from the mountains came a Great Cry. A lament of rain and storm swept aside the worn out vines, flooding the dry riverbeds and overrunning the orchards and hives. The storm lasted all that day and all that night and the people were filled with dread. Again and again they heard the fearful cry, now with lightning and thunder. On the morning of the second day the King died and his court fell silent with grief. All seemed to be lost.

Approaching the castle of the King came an old woman, bent with age, her skin grey and flaccid, her mouth thin and her teeth yellow and twisted. She carried upon her shoulder a heavy bag which, despite her age and stature, she appeared to bear with ease. Indeed, she walked straight up to the castle gate and demanded entry, banging her fists again and again on the wooden doors.

At first the gatekeeper thought that he could order her away, shouting at her through the grill of the doors and refusing her entry. But she would not go and commanded the gatekeeper to bring her before the King's council. The gatekeeper stopped shouting and listened to the old woman, for now there was something in her eyes that filled him with fear. He called for his son and sent him running to the council chamber.

At first, all but one were for setting the dogs on the old woman, but then the oldest and wisest of them spoke with the authority of his years.

"We have lost our King, the Queen has gone into the mountains and the land is wasted. Let us see what the old woman has to say."

And so the gates were opened and the old woman came before them. She strode into the council chamber pushing back the doors so that they all but leapt from their hinges. She took the centre of the floor and on it let fall her heavy bag. Slowly, she looked around, holding their attention with her eyes. And when she spoke, it was with the voice of the cold wind.

"Which of you will lift the darkness that has fallen upon this land, for if none will, all will perish? Which of you will lift this heavy bag and bear it upon his back?"

Slowly, and one by one, they came forward to pick up the bag but to their astonishment they found they could not lift it. Not an inch, not half an inch, not at all. Although the old woman had carried it upon her shoulders, it now seemed heavier than anyone could possibly bear. The court was silent and full of fear. For they felt the power of the old woman and cast down their eyes lest they catch her awful stare.

The old woman curled her lip into a sneer and pointing at them, one by one, scorned their weakness. All were caught in her contempt until, at last, her crooked finger pointed to the son of the gatekeeper and said, "There is but one among you who has a brave heart and only he will lift the bag."

All eyes turned to the gatekeeper's son who now seems drawn by the eyes of the old woman. He came forward into the centre of the chamber and grasping the bag by its neck swung it up and onto his back. As he did so, the old woman locked her hand on his wrist and pulled him to her side. No one moved and the old woman took her captive out of the chamber, out of the castle and down the road towards the mountains of the North, leaving the castle behind.

Eventually they came to a grove of trees growing around a pool of water in which rose a spring. The old woman ordered the young man to place the bag onto the ground and then to walk with her into the pool and bathe her. Without hesitation he did as he was asked, pouring the water of the spring over her and gently drawing his fingers through the twisting tresses of her hair. Step by step, she moved deeper and deeper into the pool and, step by step, he followed until, at last, he lost his footing and found himself beneath the water. Strangely he felt no fear and gave himself to the spring. It was as if he was falling into a deep sleep.

When he awoke he found himself on the bank of the pool. He stood up and looked around. The bag was there but the old woman was nowhere to be seen. He felt the warmth of the sun upon him and was soon dry. He walked over to the bag and opened it up. Much to his surprise, inside he found the cloak and the sword of the King. As he looked at them, he was aware that someone was standing at the other side of the pool. He turned and saw a beautiful maiden, clothed in the colours of the morning and carrying a flask. She knelt beside the pool and filled the flask with the waters of the spring. Then she approached him, gave him the flask and bade him put on the King's cloak and take up the sword.

He did so and from the grove of trees came two horses, one white as snow and bridled in red and the other black as the night and bridled in gold. The gatekeeper's son, who seemed now to have grown in stature, helped the maiden onto the white horse and, holding the flask of spring water, mounted the black horse which without his bidding set off down the road towards the castle.

As he came near to the castle, he could see men, women and children standing beside the road, waving their arms and holding up pots and bowls into which he poured the waters of the spring. And when he came to the castle, the gates were thrown open and there was a great crowd gathered in the courtyard crying, "Long live the King!"

Astonished at all this attention, he turned to the young maiden but she was not there. For on the white horse sat the Great Queen and in the distance he could see the blossom of the orchards and could hear the buzzing of the bee.

FINDING ELSEWHERE

THE KING'S GARDEN AND
THE WONDERS OF COMPOST

Once upon a time there was a King who had a most beautiful garden, within which was a splendid kitchen garden. The garden was tended with care and thoughtfulness by an ancient Gardener, himself the son, the grandson and the great grandson of Gardeners that had gone before. The kitchen garden was set within fine and high stone walls and it was the pride and joy of the King and the Gardener – both of whom spent as much time as they could, in the late sunshine of summer's evenings, sitting beneath the spread of a magnificent pear tree. The King and his Gardener knew every plant in the garden and at such times they would talk of the weather and of the work that needed to be done. And, in particular, they would talk of the wonders and mysteries of compost and of the compost boxes that were the particular delight of the Gardener.

But this state of peace and harmony was soon to be lost. For one day, the King was visited by the Minister of Progress on what he declared was 'urgent business'. The King received the Minister with his usual courtesy, although he had never felt altogether comfortable in his presence. And it soon became clear that the 'business' had to do with the garden.

"Forgive me for saying this, Sir," said the Minister of Progress, leaning his head to one side and smiling a little as if he were addressing a small child, "but you must see that the way in which the Gardener is managing your garden is far too old-fashioned and sets – how shall we say – well, sets a bad example. The Gardener does not in any way take advantage of the very many modern procedures and devices that have been developed and produced by my colleagues in the Ministry of All Things Modern. If you will forgive me, Sir, I have to say that his ways are – how shall I put it – well, his ways are unacceptable.

"It is most important," continued the Minister, now in full flow, "that Your Majesty is seen to be thoroughly modern, that you are – shall we say – seen to be part of all that is best in the modern world. Our focus groups have confirmed that this is so. Indeed, the very latest findings show that the people require you to be what we call a 'now person'."

The King reflected to himself that in all his long years of meeting people nobody had ever asked him to be a 'now person'. But he let this thought pass.

"The ways of the Gardener," said the King, "are the ways of his father and of his father's father. They are the ways of one who has learned to live with nature and one who has reverence for the plants and the soil."

"Yes, yes, yes," interrupted the Minister, "so you say and so you have said many times. But, Sir, if you will forgive me, we have to be realistic, we have to move on – we can hardly be expected to..."

"I am most unlikely to forgive you," thought the King. But he knew that whatever he said the Minister of Progress would not hear for, after all, he had long ago stopped listening. And so, once more, the King kept his thoughts to himself – which is more than can be said of the Minister.

"We have therefore decided," continued the Minister, "that we must get rid of the Gardener and replace him with someone from the Ministry of All Things Modern. Indeed, we have selected just the right person. He has a degree in Business Studies and has undertaken a course specialising in the economics of garden produce and leisure-management. You can be sure that before long, Sir, he will have significantly reduced the costs of your garden and increased its revenue potential. He will have at his disposal the very latest knowledge and techniques, replacing the low productivity of the hopelessly extended variety of plants at present in your garden with a more appropriate number of genetically modified species designed and engineered to give the maximum rate of return on capital employed."

And so it was that the King's garden was taken over by a Manager from the Ministry of All Things Modern. The Manager arrived with two Assistant Managers, in three very smart vans from which they took a number of sealed boxes and several large plastic containers, each one marked with a label saying

'Dangerous. Treat with Care. Keep out of the Reach of Children'. Following them came a truck from which emerged a gleaming new tractor and trailer of the very latest kind, together with an assemblage of additional parts for every possible task that the Ministry could imagine. There were cutters for cutting, diggers for digging and, most especially, sprayers for spraying.

Putting on their special protective clothing, including goggles, masks and gloves, the Manager and his Assistant Managers mounted the tractor and its trailer, now loaded with parts, and, having consulted their management plan, drove towards the kitchen garden. It took hardly any time at all to cut down the pear tree and before long the garden had been reduced to a most satisfactory state of complete flatness, which was then sprayed thoroughly with the Ministry's latest weed killer 'Stop It'. Unfortunately, some of this drifted over the wall of the kitchen garden and onto a rather beautiful clump of primroses, killing them at once. But hardly anybody noticed. At this point, the Manager and his team, having again consulted their management plan, withdrew to their vans for tea – and then left in order to be home in time to watch their favourite gardening programme, Gardening for Profit.

That evening, the King and the Gardener met at the spot where the pear tree once had stood. Neither one said a word but both understood the sorrow that they shared. Slowly anger rose within the breast of the King and he strode off to his woodshed where, picking up his sharpest axe, he rapidly reduced several large logs to kindling, after which he felt a good deal better.

And so it was that the King hatched his plan.

Calling his Gardener to him they made their way to a secret and secluded part of the garden which had long lain untouched.

"Here," said the King, "is where we will recreate the kitchen garden. For the moment, no one will know about it but, in time, when they need it, it will be here for them."

The Gardener was, of course, delighted and, with the help of his grandson, who had always liked to help his grandfather in the garden, he at once set about the task of collecting together his packets of seeds, even managing to graft a slip from the old pear tree so that it, too, would be restored. Not least, of course, he prepared his compost boxes and the magic once more began.

The next day, the Manager and his Assistant Managers returned and once again sprayed the ground, this time with a fertiliser called 'Pop-Up' that had been especially manufactured by the Ministry of All Things Modern. Following this, they began to open the sealed boxes which contained the Ministry's genetically modified seeds, including, of course, 'Big Boy' tomatoes, 'Super-Growth' cabbages and 'Speedy' beans. Each planting was meticulously recorded in the Manager's laptop computer under its defined number and with a precise record of the regime of fertiliser and pesticide to which it would be subjected. All 'creepy-crawlies' were eliminated which, of course, meant that the garden was soon silent of the hum of bees and the song of birds. This very much pleased the Manger and his Assistant Mangers who noted that it was an example of the efficiency of their system. "After all," they said, "we cannot have the bees and the birds robbing us of our harvest." Indeed, nothing moved in the garden apart from the automatic sprinkler system that from time to time switched itself off and on, again according to the Manager's master plan.

Meantime, in the Secret Garden, the Gardener and his grandson lovingly prepared the ground. They double-dug the new beds, feeding the bottom of the troughs with organic waste from the garden and well-rotted manure from the King's stables. Then they sowed their seeds, including in their planting companion plants such as marigolds and borage that would encourage the butterflies and other insects. Rather pleasingly, the birds that had been evicted from the old kitchen garden soon arrived to add their song, and water butts were put in place so that each evening the watering could be undertaken. This gave the Gardener and his grandson the opportunity to look carefully at the progress of each plant, where necessary putting in pea sticks for support or removing the occasional weed. And day-by-day, with grass clippings and vegetable waste, the compost boxes began to fill, promising in time the return of more and more goodness to the ground.

In the old kitchen garden, now firmly under the management of the Ministry of All Things Modern, everything at first appeared to be going well. Following the strict regime of the sprays of all kinds and with extensive watering, the vegetables, such as they were, grew large and shiny. As part of the newly formed business plan, trips were organised bringing busload after busload of people not to see the garden itself but to enjoy the 'garden experience' in a newly erected dome-like structure called The Virtual Garden Centre and Shop. Here many different computer-simulated rides and games were constructed, each of which enabled the visitor to see what it would be like to enter into the growing plants or indeed the soil itself and experience the process of plant growth. At the end of the 'experience', visitors found themselves disgorged into the café and shop zone where, of course, they enthusiastically purchased a great variety of products based upon the idea of a garden. Most popular of all was the rose-scented oven glove. They were also able to purchase garden produce, each vegetable wrapped in its seal-clean plastic wrapper, impregnated with the very latest taste enhancer developed, of course, by the Ministry of All Things Modern.

And so it was that one season and one year gave way to the next. Whilst the Secret Garden slowly began to blossom, the Ministry's garden not only met its profit schedule but, indeed, exceeded it. As the Minister of Progress said to the King, "You see, Sir, in the real world, price and profit are, – if you will forgive me – the measure of success. Our spreadsheets show that the return on capital in this garden is now at or above the level that can be expected for this kind of garden based upon a ten year schedule adjusted both for climate and for geographical difference."

The King was not at all sure that the Minister had any idea of what it was that he was saying. But he was far too courteous to say so and, in any event, before he could reply the Minister had spread out on the table several sheets of computer printouts that, he informed the King, were evidence of the financial success of the venture.

As it happened, that meeting took place only a day or two before the Great Catastrophe. One morning in late August a plague attacked the Ministry's garden. To the considerable astonishment of the Manager and his Assistant Manager, the cabbages began, one by one, to shrivel as if attacked by an acute case of blight. They consulted their business plan but could find nothing that would help them. And so, they consulted the Disease Control Specialists at the Ministry of All Things Modern, who were quite sure that they knew what to do.

"We must start," they said, "by a cull of the cabbages. All the plants must be destroyed and burnt – NOW!"

And so the Manager and his team pulled out all the cabbages, put them on a pyre and set fire to it. It burnt with black smoke and a foul smell. That, they thought, was that.

The next day, however, the blight had attacked the runner beans and the next day the tomato plants, the marrows and the salad crop. All visits to the garden were stopped. The sale of rose-scented oven gloves plummeted and the manufacturer went out of business, as did the companies making seal-clean plastic wrappers and taste enhancers. As day followed day, the crisis deepened and despite all efforts, the garden was soon nothing more than a wasteland – flat, barren, putrid and soaked with chemicals.

Eventually, the Manager and his Assistant Managers were transferred to a small monitoring office in a rather remote part of the Hebrides and the Minister of Progress stepped down from office to spend more time with his family, whilst it was decided that the Ministry for All Things Modern should no longer concern itself with matters horticultural. And after something of a flurry in the newspapers, the matter was forgotten.

When they had all gone away, the King, the Gardener and, of course, his grandson, who had now become a most able Under-Gardener, met in the Secret Garden. They sat beneath the now spreading pear tree and looked over the garden that they had created. They talked of the weather and of the work to be done but, most especially, they talked of the wonders and mysteries of compost and of the compost boxes that were the particular delight of the Gardener.

FINDING ELSEWHERE

THE LEAKING ROOF

A heavy rain had run through a hole in the Old Man's roof and leaked onto his floor. After he had mopped up the puddle with towels and placed buckets to catch the drips, he looked out of his window and watched the rain. He was cross about the leak and the puddle, but he could not help but delight in the rain.

And he heard Love speak to him, and she said:

Old Man, I cherish my sister Water, who brings life, for she carries me as I move within and between. She cleanses and she nourishes. She is my handmaiden, mistress and servant, all in one. She is All in One.

Wherever you look, you will find her – she is the landscape, the forest, the oceans and the tide.

Moved by moonlight, warmed by the sun, frozen into ice. She is always there. Clouds and mountains unite in Water. She serves them all; and they serve her, carrying her within. She climbs inside the trees and back down again into the roots. She buries herself in the earth.

She runs in your veins and arteries, in all your tissues, your cells, your sweat and your tears. She governs your being and rises as steam in your kettles and saucepans.

In the morning you will find her lying as dew upon the ground or as mists that cover the marshland. She drips from the leaves and rests upon the spider's web.

She runs in streams, tumbling over the rocks in patterns and vortices. She rises into the storms and falls again as rain, filling the rivers until they overflow.

But then as the clouds darkened and coldness began to bite, Love became silent.

The Old Man waited, and after a while, Love said:

And you and your kind, what have you done with this wondrous gift?

Before the Old Man could answer, she said:

I will tell you what you have done. You have broken her movement in pipes that do not let her dance. You have polluted her body with poison. You have wasted her and then you have tried to own her and put a price upon her head. You have sought to take this gift I have given to you, as if it were within your own command; as if it were yours. You have taken a wondrous gift and made it into something to be bought and sold in the marketplace. And can you understand what I have to say? I think not.

"But what can we do?" asked the Old Man, and Love replied:

If you can, in your great ignorance and stupidity, try for once to look and to listen. Try to think beyond the narrow scope of this miserable and unkind world that you have brought about. Try to see what could be if you were to set aside your greed and avarice; if you were to learn to serve instead of command. Try this.

And then the rain poured from the dark clouds and once again found its way through the hole in the roof and into the Old Man's house. He put out another bucket.

FINDING ELSEWHERE

IN BETWEEN

He waited. He knew that between the Old Story that was dying and the New Story that was yet to come there had to be a space; for without this space the New Story could not be heard.

But remaining in the space in between was not an easy thing to do. As the Old Story had begun to fall apart, those who would not, could not, bear its loss held on to it with increasing desperation. Their noise was almost deafening. At the same time a growing multitude of prophets and experts had begun to argue amongst themselves as to what it was that the New Story would be about. Each was certain of what they had found. They, too, made a great noise.

So it was not easy to sit and wait and listen. But that was what he decided to do. He had been travelling, but now he was home, comforted by being in the place he loved most, his house and garden surrounded as it was by the wide, pale and beautiful marshes of

East Anglia and the ebb and flow of the river he loved. Here it was that he began to wait.

One night whilst he had been away the river had risen and would not ebb, it had flooded over the quay and into the boat yard amidst all the boats that had been taken off their moorings for the Winter and which were now standing in the yard on great wooden blocks. A great storm, which had started far away, had swept north-eastward across the Atlantic, and the flood had come just after the time of high tide, the storm pushing the North Sea down the East Coast and blocking the flow of the ebb. He knew this was important, but could not tell why. The winds and the tide have their own story.

Waiting is not an easy thing to do, but this is where we begin, waiting in that place that lies between a story that is falling away and one that is coming into being.

For many months he had begun to live apart from what some people call 'reality' – the world described by newspapers and radio and television. He had not read a newspaper nor listened to the radio or television news for six months and had no intention of ever doing so again. He had found that this had greatly increased his sense of being present in the moments of his life, as they came and left, one moment after another and quite beyond his control. And this was the first lesson he had learnt about waiting. Waiting means not being in control, not trying to make anything happen – just waiting.

Waiting did not mean doing nothing at all; it was more like being in a state of waiting whilst doing everything else. He had been down to the boatyard, where a new boat was being built, marvelling at the craft of the boat builder, the spine of the boat set down, the planks put in place and the ribs being fitted to them. The ribs, which are steamed so that they can be bent into shape, have to be nailed to the planks before the effect of the steam wears off, each nail being bent over to hold everything in place.

And then there was his work: books to write, illustrations to be commissioned and designers and editors to speak with. He loved this work. There were telephone calls to me made and emails to be read and sent. There was food to be bought and cooked, and there was the rhythm of the day to be followed, pausing at each hour for a short time of silence. As a widower, he lived by himself, but there were grandchildren to talk to, friends to visit and Sunday lunch at the Yacht Club. And there were Arsenal and Chelsea football matches to be watched on television. Not quite the life of a hermit.

But there was always the waiting. It had become as much a part of his life as breathing in and breathing out. It had to be attended to. Waiting and waiting. Dwelling in between.

Some days he set off across the marshes, following the path he always followed, walking past the tennis courts, along the path by the allotments and then turning down the path that led to the river bank, walking along the bank and stopping to watch the river and the mud before turning back along the sea wall, climbing up the forty-seven town steps and walking back home. He walked by himself, walking with a stick and keeping a good pace. And while he walked he waited.

"Can you hear me?" said the Story. "Can you hear me?"

He listened, and faintly heard some of the words: connection, interdependence, rhythm, ebb and flow, abundance, gathering, being prepared, movement, being entangled. But as he listened he began to feel that what he was waiting for was not what the Story was about, but how it was to be told, how it wanted to be told. It was as if the Story were alive, giving shape to the waiting, wanting to be heard, waiting to be spoken.

And then one morning just before he woke he had a disturbing dream in which he could feel Earth calling out in despair and wanting to be cared for. Not just that she was sick, but that she wanted to be cared for. And he understood that the Story was not primarily about us and what we must do, it was about something else, something more difficult to discern. Something about being. He knew the Old Story was at odds with the way things are. And he could feel this intense 'wanting' of the New Story. But still he could not hear.

He had read that long ago we learnt to tell stories, and that this ability somehow marked us out and helped us to become who we are now; and that because of these stories we have been able to create imagined orders, myths, that hold us together, enable us to belong. He had read about the ways in which we have tried to live beyond the laws of Nature, and of the trouble this has brought to us; how we needed to learn once more to live within these laws.

And he had come to know Love – her coming and going. Sometimes he had felt that 'being in love' had come to an end. It was over. But then he came to know that Love could not be held or possessed, that there could be no loss, only a coming towards and a moving away. He heard Love say:

You found me. Opening your heart, you found me. Such delight. But then you tried to hold onto me, for fear you would be alone. And you lost me. That was foolish. If you let go, I am always there.

So there he was, in between, in between one story and another. Waiting. And now he knew that the story that was to be told was Love's Story.

And the he saw her walking towards him. She seemed to be wearing a long coat, somewhat drab in colour. But as she came closer and he could see more clearly – he could see that the coat was a mixture of the most wonderful colours – lavender and green, gold and a deep blue, with specks of sand and the yellow of aconite. The coat, which fell from her shoulders almost to her ankles, was made of wool pressed into a fine felt, soft and moving with her steps.

She came come close by, but although she appeared to be walking towards him, she stayed apart, the distance between them remaining the distance of four or five paces. At first he was overcome and could not move at all, but then, as if he knew how he should be, he turned and walked in the same direction that she was taking. At first she was behind him, but then she was ahead, and he followed her, matching his pace to hers.

And so they walked together and for a while he heard and saw and felt and tasted all around him with a new intensity and clarity. Everything he touched or smelt came alive and he became part of a wondrous being, full of abundance and generosity.

This might have been forever, but foolish as he was, he began to wonder and as if he were standing apart, tried to understand what it was, to find its meaning. At that moment she disappeared and, as before, he was left by himself, waiting.

A WAY OF
BEING

FINDING ELSEWHERE

WHY?

Fill your bowl to the brim and it will spill.
Keep sharpening your knife and it will blunt.
Chase after money and security and your heart
will never unclench.
Care about people's approval and you will be
their prisoner.
Do your work, then step back.
The only path to serenity.

Lao Tzu c. 604-531 BC

The Queen left the palace garden and walked across the fields to the cottage of the Old Man, hoping he would be able to answer her question. When she came to the cottage she found him sitting on a bench by the front door, his legs stretched out, his hands across his stomach and his head lifted to the sky. He was asleep.

Not wishing to disturb him, the Queen, too, sat down on the bench, being as quiet as she could and waiting for him to wake, enjoying this moment of peacefulness.

After a while, the Old Man opened one eye and then the other. He gave a deep sigh and sat up, for a moment casting his eyes down upon the ground as if he were pondering something that had come to him in a dream.

"Welcome, Your Majesty," he said turning towards her, bowing his head and smiling. "And why, I wonder have you come to see me?"

"Well," said the Queen, "all is not well in my realm. There is much suffering, not least amongst the most poor; and amongst many elderly people who, at the end of their lives, suffer for a want of care. My advisors tell me that we are doing all we can. They talk about the costs of care, a general shortage of funds and 'the need for 'austerity.' They tell me that above all else we must ensure the growth and prosperity of what they call 'the economy' and that this means supporting banks and business above all else. The gap between the rich and the poor widens evermore, but I am told that this is just about rewarding enterprise and being competitive."

"I suppose all of this must be true," continued the Queen, "but tell me, tell me why it is that whilst those who are selfish prosper and are honoured we care so little for those who are most in need of our care? And tell me why it is that we care so little for those who give us care?"

For a moment or two the Old Man said nothing,

but then he turned towards her. "Your Majesty," he said, "the answer to your question is more simple than you might suppose. The answer to your question about why we care so little for those most in need and care so little for those who take care of us is this: we simply do not care."

"That," said the Queen, is what I feared you might say. "I had hoped that this was not so. But, of course, it is."

For a while they sat together without speaking. A deep sadness came upon the Queen, who had not wanted to hear what the Old Man had told her, but knew that it was true.

"If you wish," said the Old Man, "I will tell you how it has come about, but first we must find some shelter from the sun." And as he stood up the Queen took his arm and walked with him down the path that led away from the cottage and towards a part of the garden that was set about with large shrubs and an old and splendid red oak. There, underneath the red oak, were set two garden chairs, each one having a fat and colourful cushion to sit upon.

The Queen and the old Man sat down and for a while enjoyed the coolness of the shade. Then the Old Man leant forward and again looked towards the Queen.

"From our very beginning," he said, "we have sought both to care for each other and ensure our own survival. These two have commanded our coming together and our standing apart, the first driven by love and the second by fear. Needing to love and be loved, we have come together. Needing to protect ourselves and survive, we have stood apart. For much of our lives, and the lives of our forebears, these two necessary qualities were always kept in balance, in harmony. However, somewhere along the pathway that brought us here, we decided to take another and particular direction. We had always needed to survive and we had always needed to care for each other, but the pathway that we chose shifted the balance. Fear overcame us, and out of this fear we chose to favour our own personal survival against the common good. And we invented all sorts of stories that told us this was the right thing to do."

The Old Man paused for a moment to watch two damsel flies, each with a body of blue, come to rest on the arm of his chair and then fly away towards the pond at the bottom of his garden; whilst his cat walked by, tail held high, and with a mouse in its mouth, disappearing into the bushes. The Queen remained still, wanting to hear what it was that the Old Man was saying.

"This decision," he continued, "this decision to favour our own survival, was taken a very long time ago, for even the Buddha and the great Lao Tzu talked about it. But as time has passed it has taken us further and further apart from each other, all the time weakening our capacity to care. Until now, we have come to believe that selfishness is our normal way of being; that we are by nature self-centred and brutish, ever competing one against another. Indeed, we have come to believe that our common good comes from this selfishness. That we should care for each other, that we are by nature loving beings, is thought to be quite unrealistic, something of a fantasy."

The Old Man stood up and invited the Queen

once more to take his arm, which she did. And as the sun began to settle behind the trees, they walked slowly back towards his cottage.

"The fruits of our decision have been bitter, very bitter indeed," said the Old Man as they walked together. "Because we have followed the path of selfishness and greed, we never have enough and so we have to take more and more, without limit, and this has damaged our Mother Earth. But there is something else, too. In truth, it is not easy for us to deny our natural inclination to care for each other. It causes us great distress, it leaves us with a deep and unspoken yearning for something we have lost; which, dear Queen, is why more and more of your people are ill at ease. Their dis-ease has come about because they have been asked to deny their true selves. More suffering ... "

"You know," he said, "a long time ago it was the Buddha who told that those who would live well must dwell in what he called the four 'divine abidings' of loving-kindness, compassion, joy in and for others and equanimity. To live in any other way, he said, is to live in ignorance and suffering. So, living as we do, we cannot expect anything else. Without love we cannot be who we truly are, for Love is the essence of our Being ... "

"This means that there is work to be done," said the Old Man. "We must most urgently come together as a community of those who practice love and compassion at home and at work, in our private and our public lives. We must have courage and persistence and not be put down by those who would keep things as they are. Above all, we will need friendship, loving kindness, compassion and a care for each other and for all that is – personal, communal and cosmic Love."

They had reached the Old Man's cottage and now stood by the bench upon which the Old Man had been sleeping. He bowed his head and bade the Queen "Good bye."

She thanked him and turned to walk back along the path across the meadows.

I wonder what happened. Do you think the Queen was able to find Love and ease the suffering of her people? Do you think that her Advisors came to see that there had to be a change in the governance of her realm? Or do you think they dismissed what the Old Man had said as a nonsense?

FINDING ELSEWHERE

THE PRINCESS WHO ASKED
MANY QUESTIONS

Once upon a time there lived a Princess who asked a great many questions. Why is this and why is that? What is this for and where does that road lead to? Again and again her father, the King, explained to her that as she was a girl she was not supposed to ask questions, only to be good to her mother and learn to sew.

The Princess was not at all happy with this and vowed to herself that she would find the answers to the questions come what may. But who would be her guide? She sought help from the wise men of the court, but they merely repeated what the King had said, warning her that it was well known that the female brain was smaller than that of the male and, thus, was not designed for serious talk. She tried speaking to the Archbishop, but he dismissed her with a sweep of his hand and told her that if God had intended women to think he would not have made them so short. The Princess was furious and ran out of the chapel, slamming the great wooden doors behind her.

Day after day, week after week and month after month, the Princess struggled to find the answers to her questions until, at last, one afternoon early in May she found herself sitting upon a bench in the gardens of the palace, her head in her hands and tears pouring from her eyes. She wept and she wept until the tears had made a pool on the ground beside her.

Suddenly she heard a voice: "If you do not stop crying," said the voice, "I may have to move."

Looking up, the Princess saw before her, curled upon the edge of the flower bed, a cat – her head resting on her paws, her eyes half open, watching the slowly encroaching waters.

"I am so sorry," said the Princess, and immediately took out her handkerchief and began to mop up the little puddle.

"It is of no real importance," said the cat, "but this is the warmest spot in the garden at this time of day and I would prefer to be able to stay here until the sun moves behind the tower of the chapel, when I shall have to make my way to the kitchen for supper."

"I won't cry any more," said the Princess, who had never before had a conversation with a cat, "but perhaps, if you don't mind, I could stay here with you – until, that is, the sun moves behind the tower of the chapel and you have to make your way to the kitchen for supper."

"I should be pleased to have your company," said

the cat, "although you do seem to be rather distressed."

Quite forgetting that she was speaking to a cat, the Princess began to unburden herself, telling the cat all about the things that she wanted to know and about her wish that someone would help her find the answers to her many questions. When she had finished, the cat tucked her paws beneath her chest and lifted her head to catch the last remaining rays of sunlight. The soft fur of her front was the colour of banana mousse.

"I have found," said the cat, "that the trouble with questions is that they are so very distracting. They make me feel quite dizzy. The most important thing is to be in place." And as the last beam of sunlight left the garden and disappeared behind the tower of the chapel, the cat stood up, stretched and began to walk towards the palace kitchen.

As the Princess returned to her chamber, she could think of nothing but the cat. And the more she thought, the more she remembered how she had been in that particular warm spot in the garden at that particular time of the day, how well-placed she had been to catch the rays of sunshine and how she had left the garden as soon as the sun had moved behind the tower of the chapel.

As she entered the room, the evening sun passed through her window and rested upon a chair beside her dressing table. Now, without thinking, she sat down upon the chair and enjoyed the gentle warmth of the evening light. She felt strangely calm and, for once, had forgotten all the questions that ran around inside her head. Undisturbed, she sat there until the last of the sunlight left the chamber.

The next day, in the afternoon, she returned excitedly to the garden. But the cat was not there, nor the next day, nor the next. The Princess began to wonder whether, perhaps, she had imagined her conversation. And, after a while, her questions returned to taunt her. But, each evening, she would return to her room and sit down upon the chair by her dressing table, and here, for a few moments, as she felt the sun warm upon her skin, she remembered the words of the cat. And as she did so, the questions would subside and the strange feeling of calm returned to her.

Some weeks passed and, in sorrow, the Princess was now convinced that it had all been a dream. One morning her mother, the Queen, asked if she would go to the great walled vegetable garden of the palace and collect some herbs that she needed for a nosegay. It was a beautiful, still, morning and the Princess was glad to get out of the palace. She took a small basket and a pair of scissors and set off on her task, entering the garden through the gates decorated with leaves and pineapples.

It was a beautiful garden and the Princess walked along the gravel paths, each one covered with vines and clematis that spread themselves over the rows of arches that spanned the paths. Stopping here and there to look at the vegetables, she noticed the early potatoes, the garlic, the spinach and broad beans. Then, just as she turned towards the bed of herbs, she saw the cat lying on her side between two rhubarb pots, her back leaning against the warm wall of the garden.

The Princess was so excited that her words tumbled forth like bubbles from the neck of a champagne bottle.

"Where have you been, and why have you not come back to the garden? You're not really a dream are you and where do you go when you are not here?" The questions follow one upon another until the Princess felt quite exhausted.

This time the cat said nothing but, with her eyes closed, remained very still, the soft oatmeal flow of her belly gently rising and falling to receive the warmth of the morning sun. The sight of the cat and her slow and gentle breath eventually calmed the Princess who stopped talking, sat down upon the path, lifted her face towards the clear blue sky and closed her eyes. Feeling the gentle warmth of the sun she breathed in and out.

Suddenly, she shivered and when she opened her eyes she realised that the sun had passed behind the canopy of the great horse chestnut tree that grew in one corner of the garden, and which now cast its shadow over her. She stood up and turned to the cat, but she was nowhere to be seen. Again, the Princess wondered whether she had imagined it, but there, on the ground between the two rhubarb pots and close to the wall, was the indentation left by the cat's body. And when she knelt down and placed her hand upon it, it was still warm. She picked up her basket and scissors and went straight away to the herb beds to gather the herbs for her mother's nosegay.

That evening when she came to her room and found herself once more sitting on the chair by her dressing table enjoying the evening sunlight, the memory of the rhythmic breathing of the cat and the gentle rise and fall of her oatmeal belly, returned to her. She began to notice her own breath. She watched it come in and go out, and come in and go out again. She felt the rise and fall of her own belly and noticed how her chest opened to take in the breath and how it contracted as the breath left. On the in breath she felt still and on the out breath she felt calm.

And so she sat there, undisturbed, until the sunlight left her room.

For the rest of the year that followed, the Princess and the cat met on many occasions, but always by surprise. Sometimes the cat would be there and sometimes she would not. Sometimes the Princess would see the cat sitting erect upon the top of a distant wall. And sometimes, when she turned the corner, the cat would be right there. The Princess learnt much from the cat.

She learnt about patience and about attentiveness, and she came to notice the cycles of the Moon and the changing seasons. She learnt where to shelter from the draft of the wind and how to listen for the sound of mice. On some evenings in the depths of winter, when it was especially cold outside and when the snow and rain battered against the window, she would find the cat curled into a ball, asleep upon a cushion by the fire in her room and, together, they would rest upon the breath.

And although the questions never went away, they began to behave themselves. The Princess would reflect upon one question at a time, returning to the rhythm of her breath whenever she felt lost. And if she could not find all the answers, it seemed to her that questions that had once been overwhelming and fearful now seemed at least manageable. And some just went away. She came to look forward to her evenings in her room and it was soon understood by the rest of the household that this was her time and that she was not to be disturbed.

Indeed, on several occasions when the King was perplexed about what he should do, the Princess was able to make a number of quite useful suggestions. Noticing this, the King said, "I hope you have not been worrying my wise men or my Archbishop with your endless enquiries?"

"No," said the Princess, "but I have spent time with a cat."

"Well," said the King dismissively, "I don't think anyone could learn much from a cat!"

FINDING ELSEWHERE

WASH YOUR BOWL

This story was told to me:

A monk went to see his Master and asked him for enlightenment.

"Eat your breakfast," said his Master.

"I have eaten my breakfast," said the monk.

"Wash you bowl," said his Master.

At that moment the monk received enlightenment.

FINDING ELSEWHERE

THE MERCHANT AND HIS LIST

Once upon a time, in a town by the sea, there lived a very busy Merchant. He was busy all the time. From the moment he awoke until the moment he went to sleep, he was busy. In the morning he was busy. At seven, his alarm clock rang and he immediately got up, brushing his teeth and washing himself from the top of his head to the tip of his toes. Then, without ado, he brushed his hair, put on his clothes, and tied the laces of his shoes in a double bow.

He was busy in the evening. And when it was time to go to bed, he threw off his clothes, washed, brushed, scrambled into his pyjamas and literally jumped into his bed. Then, sitting upright against large goose-down pillows, he took paper and pencil in hand and began to make a list of all things that he had to do the next day: things he had meant to do today, but had not managed to do; things he had already planned to do the next day; and then, so as to miss nothing, some things he had only just thought of. Once the list was complete, he placed it carefully on his bedside table, put down his pencil, turned onto his side and fell quickly asleep.

Every morning he followed the same routine of washing and brushing and dressing, and then, picking up his pencil and his list, strode through to his kitchen where Molly his housekeeper, who always wore a flowery apron, had already prepared his breakfast of toast and marmalade and dried apricots.

He seldom said "Good morning" to Molly or even noticed she was there. For as soon as he sat down, he looked at the list he had prepared the night before and added two or three more things that had come to him in the night and whilst he was brushing his teeth.

As soon as he finished his breakfast, he folded his list carefully and placed it in his jacket pocket. He then put on his overcoat and hat and, checking that he had the key to his front door and a spare handkerchief, he set off for his warehouse in the middle of the town, the pace of his walk making clear to anyone whom he met, or rather passed by, that this was a man of importance with things to do.

The Merchant's warehouse stood between a shop that sold all sorts of delicious foods to eat and another that sold all sorts of delicious things to drink. Opposite the warehouse was a café for teas and coffees, sandwiches and pastries, and next to that was a chemist with row upon row of potions and plasters and things that smelt of the sweetness of flowers and blossom. But these were of no concern to the Merchant, who was intent only on getting into his warehouse where, amid all the packages and parcels, he felt safe and secure.

For here was all he needed in order to complete the tasks on his list: his desk, his chair, his telephone, some pencils and a pile of spare paper upon which he wrote of things to be added to the list for the next day. When he arrived at the warehouse, Ben Snow, his manager, and Wendy Patterson, his secretary, were always there, waiting for him. But he seldom said "Good morning" or even noticed them. Instead, as soon as he arrived he took off his coat and hat, sat at his desk, took his list out from the pocket of his jacket and, having read it through, added one or two more things that had occurred to him as he had walked into the town. Then, checking the time on his clock, he started his work. He had no time for anything else and no time for anyone else.

Then one day, having risen as usual, washed and brushed and dressed as usual, had his breakfast as usual, arrived at his warehouse as usual and sat down at his desk as usual, the Merchant felt into his pocket for his list and… and… and there was nothing there. The pocket of his jacket was empty –completely and utterly empty.

This came as something of a shock. He checked the many other pockets of his jacket, but although he found a paper clip, some cough pastilles and a spare button, there was no list. This was becoming alarming.

He stood up and went to his coat. He checked the pockets of his coat. The key to the door of his house was there. His spare handkerchief was there. But there was no list … No list. No list at all.

The Merchant began to feel unwell, with sweat on his brow and his heart beating at rather a fearful pace. This had never happened before. He had never before been unable to find his list. He had never before been without his list. Reaching for the top of his desk, he made his way unsteadily back to his chair and sat down.

Then he started the process of checking again, once more going through the many pockets of his jacket and then stumbling over to his coat and once more checking its pockets, too. No list. No list. No list at all.

"I must retrace my steps," he said to himself, and so he stood up, put on his coat and hat and left his warehouse. He walked back to his house, taking the exact same route as he always did – along the High Street, up the Town Steps, down one road and then another before he was walking through the alleyway that led to his house. Through his garden gate he went, and up his garden path, all the time looking from one side to another to see if this was where he had dropped his list. No List. No List. No list at all.

He went to turn the key in the lock of his door, but it was open. He stepped in and as if on tiptoe and looking all around, made his way into the kitchen where Molly, wearing her flowery apron, was washing up and putting away the toast rack, the marmalade and the dried apricots.

She seemed very surprised to see him. For, in all

the many years she had worked for the Merchant she had never known him return home until the early evening, just before supper. And she could see from his pale face and staring eyes that something bad had happened. She was about to ask if he was alright, but he walked right past her to the table where he had been sitting that morning and went down onto his knees to look underneath. No list. No list. No list at all.

He rose to his feet and fell into his chair, all crumpled up.

"What is the matter?" asked Molly. "Whatever is the matter?"

At first the Merchant said nothing, but just sat there, staring. She waited. Nothing. She waited. Nothing. She waited again, and again the Merchant said nothing at all. But as Molly reached for the telephone to call the doctor, the police and the fire brigade, the Merchant whispered, "I have lost my list. I have lost my list. I have lost my list."

It was some while later, after Molly had made some tea and brought it to the table in the kitchen, and after the Merchant had taken a few sips, that Molly was able to enquire quite what the Merchant had meant about losing his list. Gradually, he told the story. Every night when he was in bed he made a list of things to do the next day, where and when. And then, at breakfast in the morning, he added some more things that he had just thought of, before walking to his warehouse where, having taken off his coat and hat and sitting down as his desk, he would add the other things that had occurred to him while walking into the town. But, today – well today when he had looked for his list it was not there. No list. No list. No list at all.

"Well," said Molly, trying to be helpful, "perhaps, if we sit here quietly, and if I bring you a pencil and some paper you could make the list again – you could write down all the things you thought of last night, this morning at breakfast and when you got to your warehouse?"

"That's it," said the Merchant, beginning to look a bit better. "That's it, that's it! That is it."

So the Merchant sat at the table and Molly brought him a pencil and some paper. The Merchant picked up the pencil straightened the paper and prepared himself to write down his list of things to do.

"Ah," he said, and the then, "Yes," he said and then… And then he said nothing at all. Nothing. Nothing. Nothing at all.

He had forgotten what it was he had written down at night. He had forgotten what it was he had written down at breakfast. He had forgotten what it was he had written down in his warehouse – which, of course was nothing at all, because that was when he found he had no list. No list. No list at all. Once more he began to feel unwell, his brow sweating and his heart beating at rather a fearful pace. Once more he felt his whole body crumple, and all he could do was stare across the room.

"Well," said Molly, "perhaps your list had on it the potatoes that we need for supper?"

"No," said the Merchant.

"Or the flea powder we want for the cat," she said.

"No," said the Merchant.

"Or the laundry we need to collect, or the new shirt you need, or...."

"No, no, no," said the Merchant his voice rising as he spoke. "None of these things, none of these things were on my list. I never have potatoes on my list. I never have flea powder on my list. I never have laundry or shirts or anything like that. My list is always of much more important things, things like... things like... things like..." But now he could not remember what sort of things he usually had on his list. Nothing. Nothing. Nothing at all.

For the rest of the day, for the rest of that night, and for the rest of the next day, the Merchant struggled to remember, trying all sorts of ways in which to do so. He walked around his kitchen barefoot, first clockwise and then the other way about. He took a cushion into the corner of his bedroom and sat there, cross-legged counting from one to ten, and then again, and then again. He tried to stand on one leg and breathe deeply. And so it went on. But whatever he did, he could not remember, – try as he might – he could not remember anything about his list. Nothing. Nothing. Nothing at all.

He drank a cup of tea, a glass of water and then a small glass of red wine. Nothing. Nothing. Nothing at all. He ate an oatcake, a carrot and a large almond. Nothing. Nothing. Nothing at all.

At last, exhausted and fretful he walked into his

bedroom and, without taking off his clothes or washing or brushing his teeth, lay down upon his bed. And as he lay there he fell asleep, a long and very deep sleep.

In a dream, the Merchant saw himself making a list. He saw himself adding things, straightening the paper and looking carefully at all the things to be done. But then, before he could do any of them, he crumpled up the list and lost it. In his dream he started list after list, but each time, just as he was beginning to look at it and to consider what to do next, he crumpled it up and lost it. This went on and on until, in his dream, he could hear... he could hear... he could hear laughter. At first it was faint and then it was louder and louder. And to his great amazement he began to see that the person laughing was a Merchant who at first glance looked remarkably like himself; and then at a second and a third glance was certainly himself. In his dream he laughed and laughed and laughed. He laughed from the top of his head to the tip of his toes – he shook with laughter, he ached with laughter, he was completely and entirely taken over by laughter.

And when, in the morning, he awoke, he was smiling. Actually he wasn't smiling, he was grinning. And when, as he washed and brushed and looked at himself in the mirror, he could not help but grin wider and wider and wider.

He vowed never to make another list.

Once he was dressed, taking time to button his jacket and place in his breast pocket a yellow-spotted hand-kerchief, he walked slowly into the kitchen, seeing with delight his breakfast on the table – toast and marmalade and tea and dried apricots. And there was Molly, as usual in her flowery apron.

"Good morning Molly. What a beautiful apron you are wearing," said the Merchant, much to the surprise of Molly.

"Are you alright, this morning?" she asked.

"Oh yes," said the Merchant, "I am indeed alright. But this morning I have something I want you to do. I want you to go down to my warehouse and speak to Ben and Wendy. Tell them, tell them to just get on without me as I am going to rest for the next few days."

And so she did. And so he did, not only for a few days, but for the rest of his life.

The Merchant had no need for lists. He always knew what to do, because he was doing it; he always knew where to be, because he was already there; and he was always on time because whenever he was doing it was always the right time to do it. He walked slowly and not always in a straight line, and quite often he did not get dressed until just before lunch, taking time to walk about his garden in his dressing gown and slippers with a watering can, watering his pots of tulips, talking to his silver birch trees, watching for frogs in his pond, putting seed onto his bird table, digging potatoes for lunch and supper and picking fresh mint and leaves for salad.

When he did get dressed and walk into the town, he often spoke to the people he met along the way. And he never went to his warehouse, but instead went to the café opposite, where he would sit for a long while drinking tea and eating shortbread made with salted butter and caramel. He watched people buying food and drink and visiting the chemist, wondering what it was they were buying. Sometimes he could not resist asking them, inviting them to come and sit and have tea with him, and then all sorts of conversations took place and many friends were made.

Now, even without a list, the Merchant remembered all sorts of things. Not the sorts of things that had been on his old lists, of course, but things to say to his grandchildren, the phases of the moon and the height of the tide, that snowdrops came in February and that the Painted Lady butterflies came in July. And all sorts of people and events now found their way into his life. This was for the first time because, before, they had never been on his list.

The Merchant never, ever found the list he had lost and quite soon forgot all about it. No list. No list. No list at all. But one day, emptying the pockets of her flowery apron, Molly found it. She tore it into very very small pieces and, walking by the sea, threw it over the waves and let the wind carry it away.

But that of course is NOT what happened. It is just a fantasy.

This is what really happened.

The Merchant enjoyed visiting the café and making friends with people going in and out of the shops. That is true. But after a while he began to suffer from a worrisome languor and loneliness. Sitting on his own at the café, he began to wonder what was happening in his warehouse, and borrowing a pencil and using the paper napkin, he began to jot down one or two things he might like to ask about.

Then one day, he stood up from his table and taking the pencil and the napkin with him walked across the road. Pausing for no more than a moment he opened the door of his warehouse and went in. Ben Snow and Wendy Patterson were surprised to see him, but he greeted them in a friendly way and asked if they would mind if he just sat for a while at his desk and watched what was going on.

They cleared the desk of papers, offered the Merchant his chair and asked him if he would like a cup of tea.

"Yes, please," said the Merchant, "and a biscuit if that is possible."

And so the Merchant sat for a while, sipping his tea and eating his biscuit, as Ben and Wendy checked lists, packed parcels and tied them up, placing them ready to be taken to the post office.

"What is in that parcel?" asked the Merchant.

"Boot laces," said Wendy.

"And in that one?"

"Sink plugs."

"And in that one?"

"Garden hose."

And so it went on, with the Merchant again and again adding one or two items to his paper napkin.

"I'm off now," said the Merchant, "and try not to be too late yourselves."

And then he set off home, strolling through the streets and stopping from time to time when he met friends.

When he arrived home, he spent a little time walking around his garden, adding a note or two to his napkin before unlocking the door and going in. The house was quiet and for a while he went from room to room before finding a pencil and some paper and sitting down at his table.

There were things to do and there were people to visit and there were some others he would telephone. He transferred the notes from his napkin onto a new list and then added a few more matters he had just though about.

He began his life again, making himself busy both at his warehouse and sometimes at the café, where he would meet friends. His lists became much more elaborate and extensive, with such a range of items that he would often have to rewrite them twice or three times a day.

And one day, and much to her surprise, he asked Molly to marry him. He had come to understand the comfort and the beauty she brought to him. They lived together for many years and he never quite stopped making lists and having things to do – together.

FINDING ELSEWHERE

A BOWL OF TEA

A Merchant went to visit a Hermit to seek enlightenment and knocked on the door of his hut. The Hermit opened the door, invited the Merchant in and offered him a bowl of tea. The Merchant refused. He did not like tea in a bowl. He did not like it at all. And anyway he had been taught to drink his tea from a cup. A porcelain cup with a saucer.

The Hermit said nothing. And then he said nothing again. In fact he continued to say nothing for some time. This was not what the Merchant wanted. He did not want it at all. He had been taught that it was very rude to remain silent when in the company of others. In fact he had been taught it was not good to be silent at any time. There was always something that needed to be said.

So, after a while, quite a short while in fact, when the Merchant could not bear it any longer, he said to the Hermit: "I have come to you to seek enlightenment. What have you to say to me?"

The Hermit looked at a hole in his carpet and said nothing. For a long time he said nothing. But then he said, "I am not sure I can remember."

This was not what the Merchant wanted to hear. This was not what he wanted to hear at all. He did not like it when people could not remember what it was they wanted to say to him. And anyway he had been brought up to make notes of what he wanted to say to people so that he would not forget what it was he had to say, and he rather expected other people to do the same.

He looked rather severely at the Hermit, but it had no effect as the Hermit was still looking at the hole in his carpet.

This was not what the Merchant wanted to see. It was not what he wanted to see at all. He did not like it when people looked at holes in their carpets. And anyway, he had been taught to mend his carpets so that there were no holes in them into which people could look.

The Merchant began to feel cross and after a short while began to rise from his chair.

As he did so, the Hermit began to speak.

"There was a time before. There was a time, a time before your time, when all was well. This was a time of darkness, a time before the light. The darkness holds a great mystery. The light comes out of the darkness but the darkness is always there. The darkness remains and the light comes and goes. The beginning comes from the darkness and the ending returns to it. Knowing lies in the silence and stillness of the darkness – only there. Everything that is, has come from the darkness and to it will return. Coming to be, coming to be. Ceasing to be, ceasing to be. If you would see, first close your eyes. If you would act aright, be still. If you would speak, be silent. You must learn to rest in darkness."

This was not what the Merchant wanted to hear. This is not what he wanted to hear at all. He did not like the darkness. He was frightened of it and anyway he had been taught to see in it all that was evil and bad. He preferred the light. For he had been taught that everything that was good came from the light. He even kept a light on at night-time in case he woke up in the dark.

He began to speak. But then he stopped. The Hermit was not listening to him but was bent over a brown pot into which he appeared to be pouring tea leaves from a blue tin on the shelf above the fireplace. He then left the room taking with him a large kettle and saying, "Come and see me tomorrow afternoon".

The next afternoon, after eating lamb chops and potatoes for his lunch, the Merchant came again to see the Hermit. He knocked on the door of his hut but there was no reply. He knocked again. No reply. He knocked a third time and again there was no reply.

In some irritation the Merchant turned to leave but then noticed on the doorstep an envelope held down by a round stone. He picked it up and saw that it had written upon it, 'For You'. Assuming that this must be a letter of some importance left for him by the Hermit, the Merchant opened the envelope.

Inside he found a scrap of paper, which read, 'Just wait a while'.

This was not what the Merchant wanted to read. It was not what he wanted to read at all. He did not like waiting. He was himself very prompt and he expected the same from others. And anyway he had been taught never to be idle but always to be busy. There was always something to do.

So, he screwed the scrap of paper up and put it into the pocket of his coat. He was about to leave but then thought he would just check to see whether or not the Hermit was there. So, he went to the window of the hut and looked inside. Much to his surprise he could see the Hermit sitting in his armchair, hands folded in his lap, looking down at what appeared to be a hole in his carpet. He tapped on the window. But there was no reply. He tapped on the window again, this time quite hard. But there was still no reply. He was about to tap on the window for a third time when he saw the Hermit get up from his chair, pick up his large kettle and set off towards his kitchen.

This was not pleasing to the Merchant. It was not pleasing to him at all. He did not like it when people set off with a large kettle when he was tapping on their window and anyway he had been taught never to disappear when people were trying to visit. He never did so himself and he expected the same courtesy from others.

At first he was cross but then, since it was a nice sort of a day, the sun shining and the wind light, he paused. Quite suddenly he felt rather tired. And so he sat down on a garden bench beside the hut upon which the Hermit was drying a pair of socks. He had not meant to stay there for long but for one reason or another he did. He just sat there, shaded by an apple tree, looking at a nearby pond with its water lilies and marsh marigolds, about which two damselflies were flying. Both had thin red bodies and wispy wings.

The Merchant so enjoyed sitting on the bench by the pond and under the shade of the apple tree that the next afternoon, although no-one had asked him to do so, he found himself once again sitting there, looking at the water lilies and the marsh marigolds. There were red damselflies and blue dragonflies. There were small fish. There was a ram's horn snail. In fact there were several. And once he thought he saw a newt. He returned again the next afternoon and the next. In fact it began to be part of his daily routine, coming to the garden bench outside the Hermit's hut whenever he could – which seemed to be more and more often.

Indeed, one afternoon, he was so comfortable and quiet that he fell asleep. When he awoke he found the Hermit sitting on the bench beside him. He said nothing and the Hermit asked him if he would like to come into his hut and drink a bowl of tea. Without thinking he said he would. They sat together drinking their tea, saying nothing and looking at a hole in the Hermit's carpet. They sat there until it was dark.

Four days later, the Hermit purchased a new carpet from a wandering trader who had eaten pistachio nuts and been scrubbed clean by a blind man in a Turkish bath in Gaziantep.

FINDING ELSEWHERE

THE BANKER'S TROUSERS

Once upon a time, in the City of London, there lived a banker. This was no ordinary banker, for he was the Chairman of one of the LARGEST banks in the world and he lived in a LARGE apartment at the very top of a high glass tower. One floor down from his apartment was his office and boardroom, both of which were also LARGE. Below this, on many different floors, were the banking staff – his domain. Being large was one of the main qualities of everything to do with both the Chairman and the bank. He was large, his accommodation was large and the tower was not only large, but the largest and tallest building in the City. People walking past the building and looking up to see its top shrouded in clouds would say, "What a large building." And wherever the Chairman went, he was treated as being large and important. He was driven in a large car and flown in a large plane, and whenever he stayed in a hotel during his frequent journeys to others parts of the world, he would always stay in the largest set of rooms available. People used to say, "What a large man he is." And because of this, and because he was the Chairman of a large bank, he was regarded as being of great importance. GREAT IMPORTANCE.

Not only this. Because he was regarded as being of such importance, everything he said was taken as being THE TRUTH and anyone who did not understand what he was saying was treated as being VERY STUPID. Because people did not like being thought of as very stupid, the custom grew of not questioning anything that the Chairman said. Eventually, his words were listened to with admiration throughout the City of London, and then throughout the country. From time to time he would be invited onto television to share his words with anyone and everyone. No-one really understood what he was saying, but, not wishing to be thought stupid, they pretended that they did.

"Blah blah blah," he said. "Blah interest rates, blah first tier, blah second tier, blah blah risk management, blah blah blah arbitrage, blah blah blah blah blah."

"How wise," said his colleagues.

"What insight," said the newspapers.

"How wise and how incredibly insightful," said the financial regulators.

"How extraordinarily wise and how wondrously full of insight," said the politicians. After all, no-one wanted to be thought to be stupid.

The more that the Chairman spoke, and the more his words were received with admiration and unquestioning deference, the more he was encouraged to speak about things beyond the confines of his bank. He started to speak about commerce and the economy in general.

"Blah blah blah," he said. "Blah rates of growth, blah blah free markets, blah fiscal responsibility, blah blah blah blah blah."

And, not wishing to appear stupid, people said, "How wise, how extraordinarily wise. Yes it must be so. It must be so".

And then he extended his words further, speaking about education and healthcare.

"Blah blah blah," he said. "Competitive efficiency blah, cost effective blah, margins and accounting blah blah."

Not wishing to be thought stupid, people said, "How wise, how wise. This must be TRUE. It must be TRUE.".

And the Prime Minister went on television specifically to say how much he agreed with what the Chairman said, how especially LARGE he was and how especially important, and how only very STUPID people could possibly disagree.

One university after another gave the Chairman honorary doctorates and named their buildings after him, especially when they were very large. And so it went and so it went, until whatever the Chairman said was taken as TRUE and, indeed, it was agreed that what was true could only be what he had said.

And then one day, the Chairman's PR advisor arranged that he would be filmed on national television addressing a class of primary school children, thus showing to anyone and everyone what a LARGE and IMPORTANT person he was, how even the

education of small children was within his understanding, and how no one should question what he
had to say for fear of being thought to be STUPID.

The Chairman arrived at the school and waved
at the cameras and commentators, who were all
pointing out to their viewers how VERY LARGE
the Chairman was. Then he shook the hands of the
Headmistress and all of her staff, who were lined up
in a row. As he walked towards them, the staff whispered to each other that he was indeed a very large
man, and they noticed that his face carried a smile of
what they took to be friendliness. Indeed, they felt
honoured that such a large, wise and famous man
should have come to see them. The smile was not, of
course, friendliness. How could such a LARGE and
IMPORTANT person be a friend of such insignifi-
cant people as the teachers of a primary school? He
was not smiling at them, he was smiling at himself and
thinking, "How lucky these people are that I should
come and meet them. And how much they will learn
of the world, the real world, my world, when I speak
to the children."

Not to waste too much of his time, the Chairman
was quickly led to the classroom in which were
gathered twenty small children sitting in a circle on
the floor.

"Well, children," said their teacher, "we are
honoured today to have the Chairman with us.
As you can see, he is A VERY LARGE AND
IMPORTANT MAN, and he is going to tell you
all about everything."

The children received this introduction with due
respect and wonder. Well all of them but one. One

little girl had not quite heard what the teacher had said as she had been drawing on her pad of paper – a picture of some particular roses and a particular butterfly: yellow climbing roses and a peacock butterfly. Now, looking up, she saw not a man who was LARGE, but a man who was FAT. Indeed, with her eye for the particular, she noticed that the buttons on his jacket were pulled tight, and at that very moment one of them popped off and fell to the floor.

As he had begun to speak, the Chairman was quite unaware of this small disruption.

"Blah blah blah," said the Chairman. "Small people like you blah, important people like me blah, the world out there blah, my bank is so large blah."

The children sat open-eyed and full of wonder as this LARGE and IMPORTANT man told them about everything. Well all of them but one. The little girl who had been drawing the roses and the butterfly, and who saw nothing but a fat and red-faced man, began to frown.

"Blah blah blah," continued the Chairman. "Good education blah, preparation for life blah, come to work in my bank, blah blah blah."

Frowning now more than ever, the little girl raised her hand. No one took any notice. She raised her arm as high as she could. No on took any notice. Eventually, and now frowning more than ever, she stood up, keeping her arm and hand raised high.

The teacher, evidently embarrassed by this interruption waved at the little girl to sit down. But she would not. The teacher waved again. Again, the little girl would not sit down.

"Blah blah blah," continued the Chairman. "Blah

blah blah blah blah." And then he stopped, because he found himself looking straight into the eyes of a little girl her hand upstretched and her face frowning at him.

"Ah," said the Chairman, "I see that one of you little people has a question to ask me. What is it, little girl, that you want to say?"

At first the little girl said nothing, because she saw that another button had just popped off the jacket of the fat man. But then she spoke. "I just wanted to say," she said, "that I don't understand at all what you are saying. It seems to have nothing to do with me or with the yellow climbing roses and the peacock butterfly."

There was a gasp from the teacher and from all the other children.

"All you seem to say," continued the little girl, "is blah blah blah blah blah." Now there was silence. "And in the meantime, and because you are so FAT, the buttons are popping off your jacket."

At that moment every remaining button on the Chairman's jacket popped off and his vast belly fell out towards the children who could now see nothing but a very FAT and SWEATING man. There was a short pause and then as the Chairman seemed to be going to speak again, his face now glowing red, the buttons on his shirt popped off, one after the other from the top to the bottom: pop pop pop pop pop. And then the buttons of his braces gave way and, as the teacher put her hands to cover her eyes and as the children began to giggle and laugh out loud, the Chairman's trousers fell to his ankles.

The television cameraman and the sound man, who

had been watching this collapse unfold with their cameras and microphones fixed upon him, were so shocked that they had left the cameras rolling, and so anyone and everyone who was watching the event on their television sets and on their iPads stared in amazement at what they could now see was a FAT MAN WITH NO TROUSERS ON.

Those watching included the Prime Minister and several members of his Cabinet who had been commanded to join him in the Cabinet Room to watch the Chairman addressing the school children, eager to hear what he had to say. Now they too rubbed their eyes in disbelief and looked at each other somewhat sheepishly. One by one, the members of the Cabinet slipped out of the Cabinet Room and hurried back to their Ministries, hoping that no-one would see them. Eventually, the Prime Minister, was left alone staring at the television screen until, thoughtfully, one of his secretaries picked up the remote and turned the television off.

"Would you like some tea, Prime Minister?" she asked, but he just sat there staring at the blank screen.

"Well," said the secretary, "I will just make you one, with a biscuit." And she slipped out of the room.

It would, perhaps, be pleasing to think that the Chairman never recovered from this event, that he would ever after be seen for what he was: not LARGE but FAT. But that would be to believe in fantasy. What actually happened, of course, was that the Chairman left the school by a back door and was taken to his big car, wherein he gathered his garments about him so that by the time he was back to his big building no-one noticed his disarray. He took the private lift to his apartment, where he showered before dressing again in fresh clothes with secure buttons.

No-one ever spoke of what had happened at the school. No newspaper or radio station reported it and it certainly did not appear on the television news. Indeed, when asked about it no-one could remember what had happened.

The parents of the little girl were asked to remove her to another school, as she was evidently very STUPID. Once the Prime Minister had had his cup of tea and a biscuit, he regained his belief in all the Chairman had to say and, indeed, provided funds for the repair of the Chairman's jacket, shirt and trousers. It was not long before he was again assuring anyone and everyone of the wisdom and insight of the Chairman, reminding them that he was, after all, VERY LARGE and VERY IMPORTANT, and quite beyond criticism.

The little girl grew up to be a very talented gardener and watercolour painter. She contributed to a number of exhibitions in London and New York and to a magnificent Florilegium of the plants on the garden of the Prince of Wales.

(With apologies to Hans Christian Andersen and Danny Kaye.)

FINDING ELSEWHERE

CARRANDOUR

Once upon a time, the castle of Carrandour had been a wondrous place, its walls steep and well founded, its gardens fruitful and well tended, its wells fresh and plentiful. The people of Carrandour were renowned for the quality of their fabrics, fruits and vegetables and for the fairness of their trading. Travellers would come from far away as they were always treated well, their comfort and safety being assured by the generous hospitality of the people of Carrandour. But that was another time, and ever since the King had banished the Queen, the castle had fallen into a dreadful decline. Its walls had crumbled and its water had become sour. Its traders had become mean and dishonest and travellers avoided Carrandour as they were fearful of what would happen to them if they should go there.

It had all begun one day late in the year when the Queen had come to the King in great distress. She had heard that his advisors had told him that the rules of hospitality which had governed Carrandour for as long as she knew were to be changed; that no longer would travellers be offered accommodation and shelter without payment and that there was to be a drive to reduce the cost of producing the wonderful fabrics for which the people of Carrandour were so well known. Indeed, she had heard that it was being suggested that it would be better if these fabrics were brought in from other towns and villages far way away from the castle where they could be purchased more cheaply.

"Your Majesty," she had said when she came into his chamber, "Your Majesty there is something troubling me that I must talk about with you."

"Ah, my dear Queen," replied the King, "what could possibly be troubling you? Is it not a sunny day and are not the people content and busy? And you, my dear, what could possibly have happened to you that is so troubling? Come and sit beside me and tell me all about it."

And with that he arranged for some beautiful cushions, covered in the fabrics for which Carrandour was so famous, to be set beside him, if somewhat below him, so that the Queen could tell him what was wrong. He smiled and asked her to sit upon the cushions.

To begin with, as the Queen began to speak, the

King continued to smile, albeit that he did not appear to be listening very much to what the Queen was saying. But gradually, as she began to give the details of her concern, the smile ceased and the King looked more and more annoyed until he stood up and interrupted her.

"Really," he said, "this is most irregular. I had expected you to speak of something to do with your garden or your clothes or even your needlework. I did not expect you to be interfering in matters that are within my command; things that you cannot possibly understand, and which are no business of yours."

But the Queen was not to be dismissed. "My life," she said, "is dedicated to this castle and to the people who live and work here. It is dedicated to all that happens within the walls of the castle and to all that happens in the lands that make up our realm: the pastures and the rivers, the woodlands and gardens, the hives of our bees and the scratching of our hens. All of this is my concern, because without all of this neither you nor I have any place to be."

"Such nonsense," said the King. "How can you possibly understand these things? Have you sought the advice of my Treasurer? Have you understood the rules of economy and trade as explained by the Bankers who govern our realm? Do you know how it is that loans are made and repaid? Have you any idea at all of the rules of competition and market efficiency; the rules of marginal returns and effective cost planning?"

"And have you?" said the Queen, now flushed with anger. "Have you any understanding of how it is that we have become so loved by the travellers that visit us and by our craftsmen and those that spin and weave our wondrous fabrics? And have you any idea of how it is that by giving and receiving we have held the life of our people in harmony for all these years?"

"Harmony, love, giving and receiving! Have you gone mad?" shouted the King, now pacing around his room in great agitation. "Have you gone completely mad? You need to hear what my advisors say about what we call 'the real world' and then you will see how foolish you are."

And with that he rang a large bell standing on one of his tables. Almost immediately, a servant came stumbling through the door buttoning up his jacket.

"Get me my Treasurer and my Bankers and bring them here at once. At once!" shouted the king, and the servant hurried out of the chamber.

Moments later a small crowd of rather fat men, each one wearing the black robes and purple hats of the Special Advisors to the King, came bustling into the chamber, led by the Treasurer whose robes were lined with gold. They bowed low to the King and they smiled at the Queen with the kind of smile that betokens that someone is of little importance.

"Your Majesty," said the Treasurer, evidently aware that the King was in a state of great agitation, "Your Most Magnificent Majesty, how may we help you?"

"You may help me," said the King, "by explaining to the Queen how it is in what we call 'the real world', why it is that we must change our way of trading and why it is that we must make new rules governing the making of our fabrics and the way in which we accommodate travellers to this castle."

The fat men formed themselves into a line before

the King and with his consent sat down upon some gilded chairs that had been brought into the chamber, each one covered with a cushion made of the wondrous fabrics of Carrandour. The Treasurer remained standing and with another somewhat condescending smile turned towards the Queen. Sighing as if he had been asked to explain something rather complicated to a small child, the Treasurer began.

"Well, now, Your Royal Highness, this is all rather difficult to explain in simple terms, but if I might try to do so in words you would understand, let me say this." Another sigh. "In what we like to call 'the real world' – in the world of economy and commerce – there are rules, you see, rules that govern how everything must be, and rules that we must obey if we are to be efficient and effective and if we are create conditions in the market place that will enable my colleagues here, the Bankers, to be able to do their work in conditions that please them." At this the fat men sitting behind him on the cushioned chairs nodded and smiled.

"These rules," continued the Treasurer, "govern the ways in which prices are set and costs are controlled. And because we are always looking for what we like to call 'competitive advantage', we are always seeking to reduce what we like to call 'marginal costs and price efficiency'. We are reluctant to lend to people who cannot provide the proper collateral and frankly, Your Royal Highness, the people of Carrandour have very little to offer us. Their work is wonderful, but it takes too long and costs too much. They have hardly any assets at all and so we cannot really lend them the money they say they need to maintain their looms.

They simply do not seem to understand our rules. And the idea that travellers should be made welcome at little or no cost – fed, given wine to drink and a bed for the night without a proper payment – is so far outside our rules that we shudder to think what is happening." At this, the fat men sitting on the cushioned seats behind him again nodded and smiled.

The Treasurer was about to say more when the Queen stood up and interrupted him.

"My dear Treasurer," she said, "I know you think I am very stupid, but let me ask you one or two questions. You seem to know so much about the economy and the rules of the market place and what you like to call 'the real world', but have you ever grown vegetables?"

The Treasurer seemed somewhat taken aback and flustered. "Well," he said, "as it happens I haven't ever grown vegetables, but I..."

Again the Queen interrupted. "And have you ever worked at a loom or drawn water from one of our wells or set up a stall in the market place?"

Again the Treasurer looked uneasy. "Well," he said, "as it happens I haven't ever worked at a loom, drawn water from the well or set up a stall, but I..."

Again the Queen interrupted. "And have you ever offered hospitality to the travellers that come to our castle, made them comfortable in your home or fed them and given them wine?"

At this point, as the fat men behind the Treasurer began to mutter amongst themselves and as the Treasurer turned towards them and raised his hands in despair, the King stood up. He was clearly not pleased with the discussion.

"I must thank you," he said to the Treasurer, "for trying to make clear how things are, but if you would leave us now…"

And with that the fat men and the Treasurer bowed low and left.

"Never in all my life," said the King, "have I been so embarrassed. How can you possibly question what is said by my Treasurer and by my Bankers? It is unforgiveable that you have done this. And now you will be punished! Punished, punished, punished! I cannot have in Carrandour anyone who questions the authority of my Treasurer and my Bankers."

The Queen said nothing.

"You are to be banished from Carrandour," said the King, his voice dropping to a cold whisper. "You are to be banished."

The next day, in the early morning and before anyone had woken, the Queen left the castle, walking deep into the countryside.

Advised by his Treasurer and his Bankers, the King closed down the weaving looms and gave orders for fabrics to be brought to the castle from far away. And so it was. But the quality of the fabrics were poor and soon travellers stopped coming to Carrandour, where, in any event, they were no longer made to feel welcome.

A Great Gloom and a Great Lethargy fell upon

the people. Their orchards and vines fell into disrepair, as did the walls of the castle. The land became sick and the wells sour. Only the Treasurer and the Bankers seemed to prosper as they extended their lending beyond the castle and into far away places where trade remained prosperous.

Some years later as poverty captured the castle and the King fell ill, the King sent a message to the Bankers saying that he wanted to speak to them. But they had gone. There was nothing left for them in Carrandour.

It is said that some of the people of Carrandour left the castle and brought themselves to the Queen. It is said that a new community gathered together there, a community which cared for the Queen and was guided by her. Some say that the people built themselves looms and started to weave beautiful fabrics, and that travellers came to trade with them, marvelling at their work and being received with gentle hospitality. It is said that new orchards and new vines were planted and the people found a sweet spring that still provides them with water. It is said that they liked to call this 'the real world'.

FINDING ELSEWHERE

THE SMILE

One day some while ago, kneeling in meditation, quiet and still, an Old Man opened his eyes and smiled. Then he laughed out loud. "So this is it," he said, "and all the rest is illusion." He laughed and laughed and laughed.

FINDING ELSEWHERE

THE QUESTION

Feeling lost and tired and not knowing what to do, the Old Man went to bed. Was it the storm that had blown up the river and across the marshes? Had this made him unsettled? Whatever it was, in the early evening he had gone to bed. Sitting there, wrapping his duvet about him and closing his eyes, he called upon Love: "Tell me," he asked, "tell me how our story ends." He sat there for a long time hoping to hear her voice. It began with a whisper.

This is not a small thing you ask for and it may be you will never know, but if you wish to hear me you have to stop and listen. I cannot reach you unless you come towards me. You are too far away. Can't you see? Can't you see that unless you stop and move towards me we will become further apart? And then you will be on your own without me. Have you thought about that? Have

you thought how it will be, living without me –
living without love?

Her voice rose, and the Old Man could now hear her
more clearly.

I have tried, I have tried to reach out towards you,
but you have always turned away. Surely you can
see that. Surely you can see what is happening. If,
for a moment, you could stop and look at where
you are, surely you would see? I know you would,
but then you close your eyes or turn away as if
you cannot bear what is being shown to you, what
is being asked of you. Fear takes hold and you
turn away.

It is easier to blame the poor than love them
into being. And how can you meet violence
with violence when you can see that it always
leads to more of the same – again, again, again.
And why do you need more when you have
enough? Stop and listen and look. Why do
you think that there is so much silence around
you and within you? Why do you think that
all that is moves in a silent rhythm? Why do
you think everything is connected by silence?
Surely you can see it is because I move and am
in this way. Without silence, without stillness,
without the rhythm and without the connection, I cannot be. If you are always making a
noise and breaking things apart, if you always
separate, you will never find me. As if it were
possible for you to govern yourself without me,

you follow your own laws and have turned away from mine."

And then her voice was gone and the Old Man was left alone, sitting in his bed. He put his earphones into his ears and listened to Leonard Cohen singing The Tower of Love. In the background Charley and Hattie Webb, 'the sublime Webb Sisters' are singing, "Doo-dum-dum-dum-da-doo-dum-dum. Doo-dum-dum-dum-da-doo-dum-dum." As Cohen comes to the end of the song he speaks to his audience in his deep, dark voice as they, in turn, shriek out to him:

"Tonight it's become clear to me ... Tonight the great mysteries have unravelled and I've penetrated to the very core of things ... And I have stumbled on the answer. [They shriek at him.] And I'm not the sort of chap who would keep this to himself ... Do you want to hear the answer? ['Yes' they cry.] Are you truly hungry for the answer? ['Yes' they cry.] Then you are just the people I want to tell it to ... because it's a rare thing to come upon this. I'm going to let you in on it now ... The answer to the mysteries: Doo-dum-dum-dum-da-doo-dum-dum."

So that is it:Doo-dum-dum-dum-da-doo-dum-dum.

And in the notebook by his bed, the Old Man finds a text, which he had forgotten about. "To be internally silent," it says, "do not think too much. Trust yourself. Trust others. Trust life. You will find it easier than it seems."

You will find it easier than it seems ...

He remembers the translation of Nagarjuna's words in Stephen Batchelor's *Verses From the Centre*:

> In seeing things
> To be or not to be
> Fools fail to see
> A world at ease

> A world at ease …

Later, the house of his dearest friend with whom he sometimes stays, is flooded in a great storm, with rain that falls from the sky in such a deluge that nothing can be done to stop it. The last time this had happened was nearly one hundred years before. Everything has to be thrown away and he knows there will be weeks and weeks of cleaning and drying.

"You see," said Love, "what happens?"

"I see," said the Old Man and he asks his friend if his bed could be moved to a higher floor.

It was difficult to understand why the Other People could not see. He had tried to talk to them about the loss of Love, but they wouldn't listen. They told him that he was a fool and that the people who really knew, Really Knew, had long ago turned away from Love, making places for Fear to come in. People were fearful of not working, fearful of losing their money, fearful of not having enough, fearful of being ill and dying. Making the economy grow was all that mattered.

Sometimes the burden seemed too much to bear.

"Coming to be coming to be; ceasing to be, ceasing to be."

A world at ease.

"Doo-dum-dum-dum-da-doo-dum-dum."

FINDING ELSEWHERE

MERLIN AND NIMUE

"Come Nimue, come and be beside me. I asked for you to come. Or did you find me? It matters not. Come Nimue."

Merlin brought Nimue into his garden and they sat together on an old wooden bench as the damselflies settled on the ivy.

"Wait here Nimue, wait here." And Merlin walked into his house, returning with a box tied about with string.

"This is for you Nimue. Do not open it until I have gone. All that I am is in this box. All that I have seen and known. It is for you."

She took the box from him, placed it on the ground and walked into the garden, watching the red damselflies. When she came back, neither the house nor Merlin were there. Both had gone. But the box was by the bench where she had left it.

When she undid the string and opened the box, Nimue found inside the dried petals of a cream rose and a spiral shell.

At once she knew all that Merlin had ever known.

MERLIN AND NIMUE

FINDING ELSEWHERE

ERIC, ENID AND THE DONKEY

A story inspired by *The Mabinogion* and the tale of 'Gereint and Enid'

In the time of King Arthur and the Round Table, a young knight called Eric decided to set forth on an adventure. Quite what the adventure would be he did not know, but he saddled his horse, put on his finest clothes with a breastplate, a sword and a spear and packed upon the back of a donkey sufficient provisions to enable him to venture into the darkest forest without fear. Naturally, he was quite frightened about what it was that he might find, but determined to be the brave knight he had always been told he should be, he gathered himself together and tying the rein of the donkey to his saddle he mounted his horse.

Just as he was about to leave, Guinevere, the Queen

consort to Arthur, came up to him holding the reins of a horse upon which sat a young woman called Enid. Guinevere stood by and Enid asked Eric if she could accompany him. Not seeing what she could possibly contribute to the adventure, Eric dismissed her request outright.

"No, of course you cannot accompany me," he said. "You would simply be in the way, and you might get hurt."

"But, I will not be in your way at all," insisted Enid, "and I feel certain that you would protect me whatever happened." Appealing to his protection was, of course, very flattering to Eric, as he saw himself exactly in that role. And Enid was very beautiful.

So, pretending reluctance, Eric agreed that she could come with him provided, and this was most important, provided she rode behind him and said nothing to distract him from his quest – whatever that quest might be. Furthermore, it would be best if the donkey were tethered to her horse, leaving him free to look ahead and be ready for whatever danger they might encounter.

And so they set off, Eric in the lead, head held high and his left hand set jauntily on his hip. Enid followed, speaking kindly to the donkey, who felt sure that whatever it was they were about to do it would probably be much less enjoyable than everyone thought.

After a while a while, they came close to a dark forest. Suddenly, although Eric was looking the other way and could not see them, Enid saw four knights riding out of the forest and towards them at great speed. Remembering that she was meant to remain silent, Enid was not sure what to do, but certain that Eric was in danger she urged her horse forward until she came close to him and called out, "Beware Eric, there are four knights in armour riding at great speed from out of the forest towards us, and I fear they harm you."

"I thought I told you to say nothing to me," said Eric, and turning is in his saddle, he faced the knights and prepared for battle.

"I knew this was not going to go well," thought the donkey.

One after the other as the knights bore down upon Eric, who let their spears glance past him, delivering his own blow so that each one in turn was thrown out of his saddle and on to the ground, groaning with pain and then fleeing lest they be struck again.

"Let me tell you once more," said Eric, reining in his horse and coming back to Enid and the donkey. "Remember, I am quite capable of looking after myself without any help from you. So, silence from now on, if you please." And with that he set off again, his head held high and his left hand set jauntily upon his hip.

Enid and the donkey followed on behind.

"This will happen again," thought the donkey. "I have seen this sort of thing before, and I am sure there is more to come."

After a while, and having left the forest behind them, Eric, Enid and the donkey came to a wide plain in the midst of which was a tangled copse. Eric had his eyes set far away onto the horizon, but Enid, ever mindful of danger, looked toward the copse. And there they were, three knights in full armour setting out towards them to do them harm.

Enid urged her horse and the donkey forward until she came alongside Eric.

"Excuse me," she said, "but have you seen the three knights riding towards us from out of the copse? They seem set upon doing us harm."

Eric turned to look and saw the danger coming towards him. "How many times do I have to tell you?" he said to Enid, "of course I can see them and I don't need you to tell me. Hold your tongue." And with this, he reined in his horse, lowered his spear and prepared for battle.

"I said this would happen," sighed the donkey somewhat wearily.

The three knights were riding at great speed towards Eric, but as each one came he let their spears glance by and, striking with force, set each knight upon the ground. They scrambled up and fled lest they receive another blow.

Seeing the knights fleeing from him, Eric brought his horse up to Enid and the donkey. "I don't know how many times I need to tell you this," he said, "but I will say it once again. I do not need your help in this adventure. I just need you to follow behind and take care of the donkey. Do you think you could possibly do that?" And he turned his horse forward and set off again, his held high and his hand set jauntily upon his hip.

Enid followed speaking gently to the donkey to make sure that all was well.

Leaving the copse behind, Eric, Enid and the donkey travelled through open country until, in the distance, they could see a large forest ahead of them. Again, Eric had his eyes upon the horizon, but Enid, ever mindful of danger, looked towards the forest. As they drew closer, she caught sight of five knights in full armour, their horses with nostrils flaring, riding with speed towards them. It was evident that Eric, his head held high, had not seen them. And so, once again, Enid urged her horse and the donkey forward.

"Here we go again," thought the donkey, who liked to travel at a steady walking pace without constantly being made to run. Coming alongside Eric, Enid touched him on the shoulder, startling him. "I know you have asked me to say nothing," she said, "but I do think I should point out that there are five knights charging towards us from out of the forest."

"You are the most irritating of women,' said Eric. "You seem to be unable to do as you are told. Of course I have seen them. Please go away and be quiet!"

"I am not sure how much more of this I can take," thought the donkey.

Well, of course Eric had not seen the five knights. But now he had been warned, he turned his horse towards them and lowered his spear. Again, skilful as he was, as each knight came upon him, he let their spear glance past and delivered such a forceful blow that one after the other they were lifted out of their saddles and fell upon the ground. Seeing that they were defeated they got up as best they could and fled, their horses following them.

Tired by all of the battles of the day, Eric stood for a while, watching the fleeing knights until they were no more than a cloud of dust in the distance. Still not clear as to his Quest, he turned again towards to Enid and saw her standing beside the donkey, feeding him sweet hay from one of her saddle bags, which were embroidered with sprigs of columbine and roses. He knew that he, too, must eat and rest.

Understanding his need, Enid, spoke.

"I wonder whether we might find some place to rest?"

"You don't have to tell me that," said Eric, cross that she had once more broken her silence. "I am at this moment wondering just where the best place would be."

Of course, he had no idea where they might find a place to rest, but he set forward in the direction of the forest with Enid and the donkey following behind.

"Why don't you tell him, Enid?" thought the donkey to himself. "After all, you know what will happen."

"Forgive me for suggesting this, "said Enid, "but I think we might find rest if we were to enter the forest just over there by that old beech tree."

"That is exactly where I was going," said Eric, secretly grateful that Enid had found the way.

"Thank goodness for that," thought the donkey. "I have had quite enough for one day."

Soon, they had entered the forest and found, just beyond the beech tree, a soft patch of ground covered with leaves and overhung by braches. The donkey was tethered with a small pile of sweet hay, and Eric and Enid rested their heads upon their saddles, each covered with a blanket. Soon Eric was asleep, but Enid remained awake, keeping watch.

As dawn began to light the sky, Eric awoke to find beside him a flask of water and a slice of walnut cake, which he drank and ate without thinking quite how they might have gotten there. Enid had found a fresh stream nearby and had washed her face and given water to the donkey, who was grateful.

"Now, we must set off again," said Eric, not knowing quite what that might mean. "And remember, keep your silence."

And with that he placed his saddle on his horse, tightened the girth and mounted. Enid followed and so did the donkey, thinking to himself, "Well, I hope today is better than yesterday, although I doubt it will be."

Eric really had no idea where he was going nor what it was that his quest would be, but he felt as long as his head as held high and as long as his hand was set jauntily upon his hip all would be well. And this time he asked Enid to take the donkey and go on ahead so that she would no longer distract him from his task.

"He has no idea where he is going," thought the donkey as he and Enid led the way. "Thank goodness for Enid."

Eric let Enid find the pathway, without saying this was so, but rather looking about him in a manner he thought was befitting for a brave knight.

Enid led them across open countryside, where farmers and their families were cutting hay and gathering it into stooks. At one point, she stopped to talk to a woman binding the stooks of hay together and replenished her bag for the donkey. On they went until, in mid-afternoon, they came upon an orchard surrounded by a high hedge. Arriving first, Enid waited for Eric to catch up and then said to him, "Eric,

I think this is the place you have been looking for."

Thinking it most unlikely that all of his journeying would have been to arrive at an orchard rather than a castle or a palace, Eric drew his horse to a stop beside her. And he was about to chastise her for leading him in the wrong direction when a mist came upon him, settling over and around the orchard. With the mist was a coldness that seemed to stop the blood.

Eric was frightened, but as neither Enid nor the donkey seemed to be so, somewhat reluctantly he allowed them to lead him through a gateway and into the orchard, which bore apples of all kinds. Leaving the horses behind them, they moved forward on foot, without a word. In the middle of the orchard stood a chapel with a sloping roof and a wooden door. Enid was standing by the door with the donkey and, with the palm of her hand, signalled to Eric that he should enter. He did so, going in alone and leaving Enid and the donkey outside.

Entering into the chapel, which was lit by many candles, Eric was overcome by the scent of incense burning in a number of brass bowls hanging from the curved ceiling of the chapel. The light was dim, and to begin with Eric found it difficult to see where he was, but as his eyes became used the darkness he saw that in the centre of the chapel there was a wooden table upon which lay a young woman. Still standing by the door, he could not see her face, but he could see that she was clothed in a most beautiful gown of white with flowers and other plants embroidered upon it. The folds of the gown appeared to move as they fell towards the floor of the chapel.

The young woman seemed to be asleep, and as he

moved nearer Eric could see the gentle rise and fall of her breath within her breast. Without thinking, he knelt before the table and as he did so the chapel came to life, with tendrils and branches moving along the walls and up and into the ceiling and with many small birds and insects flitting this way and that, but in complete silence. All the battles of the previous days now seemed as nothing to the rhythm and pattern of the chapel. It was as if some divine energy, some vibrating presence, had overtaken him. As he knelt there, he saw that his sword and his spear had gone from him, his armoured breastplate had fallen away and he was now clad in light and soft clothing the colour of every season. Quite unsure of himself, he stood and turned to leave, but as he got to the door a voice called him. He turned back and as he did so, the young woman arose and stood before the table, her gown mingling with the flowers and with the wings of the insects and the birds in the chapel. It was Enid.

Nothing was said, but Eric, who now saw Enid as if for the first time, came to her side and took her hand in his. Together they walked out of the chapel and Eric took coats from his saddle bag, putting one over the shoulders of Enid and one upon himself. He mounted his horse and helped Enid to mount and sit behind him, her arms around his waist and the donkey tethered to his saddle.

"I wonder what he made of that," thought the donkey to himself, glad at last to be on the way home.

Together, Eric, Enid and the donkey made their way back to the court of King Arthur where they were first greeted by Guinevere, who had been expecting them. Now renowned for all of his adventures, Eric took his place at the Round Table and Enid sat with Guinevere. Nothing was said of the orchard and the chapel, but from that time on and for the rest of their lives Eric and Enid were never far apart and lived together and loved each other as if they were one.

"Thank goodness that's all over," thought the donkey as he settled himself in his stable and began to eat the last of the hay that Enid had brought to him.

ERIC, ENID AND THE DONKEY

FINDING ELSEWHERE

THE RIVER AND THE KING

Once upon a time there lived a great but unhappy King, for he had grown tired and the birds in his garden would not sing. Day by day the sadness grew until one day he called his physician and said to him, "You will have seen I have grown tired and that the birds in my garden have stopped their song. What can I do to recapture my love of life?"

The physician looked at the King for little more than a moment and then, taking him by the hand, led him to the window of his chamber. "Oh King," he said, "look out of your window and tell me what you see."

The King looked and said, "I see a Great Mountain at whose foot stands a Dark Forest."

"What you must do," said the physician, "is to make a journey to the Great Mountain and in the centre of the Dark Forest you will find a river. Take with you a bowl, and when you come to the river fill it with water and pour it from the top of your head to the tips of your toes. This will bring back your love of life and the birds in your garden will sing again."

And so the King prepared himself for his journey, taking with him a large china washing-bowl wrapped upon his back in a shawl decorated with roses and with tassels threaded with red beads. He walked and he walked and he walked until he reached at first the edge and then the centre of the Dark Forest that stood at the foot of the Great Mountain. But there the King found not a river but a dried-out riverbed. Feeling that all was now lost, the King knelt down and unwrapping the bowl from its shawl held it above his head as if in supplication, longing for the river. As he did so, he was transformed into a mighty rock and the bowl into a deep and dry pool.

At the other side of the Great Mountain there lived a Princess and she was beautiful, with dark black, flowing hair. She was knowledgeable in many things and was skilful in the arts of painting and music. But despite all of this she was unhappy. For she did not know where she should go or what she should do. She was forever restless, moving from one thing to another.

One day she called her physician to her chamber and said, "You see how restless I have become and how sad. Tell me what it is that I must do to find my true self."

The physician looked at the Princess for little more than moment and then, taking her by the hand, led her to the window of her chamber. "My dear Princess," he said, "look out of your window and tell me what you see?"

The Princess looked and said, "I see a Great Mountain at whose foot stands a Dark Forest."

"What you must do," said the physician, "is to make a journey to the Great Mountain and there you will find a spring amongst a grove of trees, with water bubbling from the ground. Sit beside the spring and refresh yourself from its waters. When you have done this, you will find yourself, you will find your true destiny."

So the Princess prepared herself and set off on her journey, wrapping herself in a shawl decorated with pomegranates and with tassels threaded with yellow beads. She walked and she walked and she walked, climbing the paths of the Mountain until she reached the grove of trees. But she could find no spring with water bubbling from the ground. All she could find was a dried out patch of mud from which, perhaps, a spring had once run. The Princess was desolate and, sitting down beside the muddy patch of ground, began to cry. Tear after tear fell from her eyes, and as they struck the ground she was transformed into a stream; and as a stream she began to flow down the Mountain, all the time moving this way and that until she became a river rushing and turning into the Dark Forest.

She ran through the Forest, tossing and turning, until she came upon a mighty rock, and there her waters fell into a deep and dry pool shaped like a bowl. For a while, as the waters settled in the pool, there was a great sense of peace and restfulness. The waters of the pool rose until they o'er-spilled its rim and continued on their way down and through the Forest and beyond.

And as the river passed, the King awoke and, to his delight, found himself sitting beside a deep pool of water. He took his china bowl and filled it to the brim. He poured the water over himself, from the top of his head to the tip of his toe, and as he did so he felt wonderfully refreshed. For a day and a night he rested by the pool.

The next morning, The King arose and began to retrace his steps out of the Forest and back to his castle; and as he walked and came into his garden he could hear the birds singing. He went to his chamber and placed the china bowl upon a table beneath his window, covering it with the shawl decorated with roses and with tassels threaded with red beads.

And from that day to this, whenever the King feels sad or the birds in his garden stop singing, he goes into his chamber, removes the shawl, and looks into the bowl. For in it he sees the reflection of water. Sometimes he also thinks he sees the face of a Princess, beautiful, with dark black, flowing hair. The reflection of the water and the face in the bowl bring him joy, restore his love of life and bring back the song of birds into his garden.

And what, you may wonder, happened to the Princess? Nobody really knows, but it is said that the river which runs through the Forest runs on and into the sea. It has also been said that from time to time a beautiful mermaid with long black hair has been seen resting on a rock close by the shore.

And you might wonder how it is that I know all of this. Well, it so happens that on the day the King and Princess entered the Forest, I too was there and I watched and saw all that happened. And when

they both had gone, I too knelt down beside the pool.
There I found a scrap of paper lying beside the pool
upon which were written these words:

O bowl of rock
Why do you wait,
Cupped hands of stone?
I long for water to fill the brim
That I may over flow.

O river
Where did you go
Your water rushing?
I seek the silence of the bowl
That I might rest a while
And flow.

FINDING ELSEWHERE

SHELLS

Once upon a time a brother and a sister lived together with their parents in a house by the sea. They were inseparable. She would call to her brother and together they would go to the seashore where she would sit for hours and listen to the wind and the tide whilst he went looking for sea shells, collecting them together and comparing their size and colour. As the day came to an end, he would bring his shells to his sister who would marvel at them, holding them in the fold of her apron. Day after day they played together and life was good, very good.

And then one day when the brother had finished collecting the shells and had brought them to his sister, he would not let her hold them in her apron, but insisted that she place them one at a time on the sand and look at each one separately. "How else," he said, "can you understand how each one of these shells is made?"

"I am not trying to understand them," said his sister, "I am just looking at them."

"That is no use at all," said her brother. And so they set off home going their separate ways.

For a while they played separately.

And then one day the brother fell ill and could not go down to the seashore. His sister went and sat and looked at the sea. At that moment, the breeze whipped up the sea and in the tumult a wave brought to her feet a wondrous collection of shells. She picked them up and, folding them in her apron, took them back to the house and showed them to her brother.

Sick as he was, the brother simply looked at the shells and, for the first time saw their beauty.

When the brother recovered, he asked his sister to take him down to the seashore, and there, together, they played. Sometimes he would watch as she collected shells in her apron. And sometimes she would ask him about one shell in particular.

Together, they were most content. Life was good, very good.

SHELLS

FINDING ELSEWHERE

THE WIDOWER KING

Body to fire, ash to water, spume to air
so the elements confuse and quicken.

What once had moored love's presence
is visible no more among the waves.

The boat's bow dips one last farewell:
yours the life left on the shore.

'On Aldeburgh Beach: For David' from *Far from
the Dawn: Poems 2013 and 2014* by Brian Keeble

The King had gone to bed, but could not sleep. Something was shifting. Something that had started three years before was beginning to come loose and beginning to shift.

He had not meant it to happen, but it had. One day in December, at around lunchtime, the Queen had died and was gone forever. And the King was left behind. In that moment, in that instant, his world had changed. He remained a King, but now he was a Widower.

But although he was a King, and although he remained in his castle, and although he had many Advisers in his court, he had never been a Widower before and no one had told him how this would be. He had been a young man when he had married the Queen, only twenty-five years old, and over a great many years in her company, he had learnt how to be a King with her. Now she had gone and he was by himself, a Widower King.

He pulled his duvet up to his chin and turned onto his side, but still he could not sleep. For the first two or three years after the Queen had died, the King had somehow overlooked his loneliness. Being a King, of course, meant that there was always something to do. There were meetings with Ministers and meetings with Ambassadors. There were new flowerbeds to be planted, and then solar panels on the roof. There were visits to be made and guests to be received. Each day was set about with things to do and people to see. And so the years had passed – not content but making do, being a King.

The King had been advised by his Ministers, none of whom, as it happens, had ever been a Widower, that the second anniversary would be 'a turning point'.

"Once, Sir, you reach this point," they had said,

"you will recover, and you will be yourself once again."

But that hadn't happened. In fact, as the King now recalled, at that second anniversary the emptiness seemed deeper than before. And now, lying alone in his bed, with the third anniversary approaching, the emptiness remained, and he began to see, as if for the first time, that this was how it was and that this was how it was always going to be. Forever. He was going to be a Widower King living by himself forever. Forever.

Sitting up, turning on his bedside light, and looking at his cat, Tinkerbelle, curled in her basket on the blanket box at the end of the bed, the King now felt quite suddenly that this was most peculiar – that this was not at all what he had expected. For the first time in his life he was by himself. He would go out and come back. He would host a meal or receive a guest. He would spend some time with his family or his friends. And then, when they had all gone home, he would once again be by himself. The sadness, the loss, the emptiness had not gone away. It had remained. When he returned from a visit to another part of his realm, the Queen was not there to welcome him. She was not there when he sat down to supper and she was not there when he walked in his garden. And this was how it was going to be. Forever.

And then as a strange sensation began to arise within his chest, he realised that he was frightened. Close by, but not showing itself, there was something that frightened him, frightened him very much.

The King got out of bed, put on his dressing gown and slippers and under the watchful but sleepy gaze of his cat, walked to and fro in his room. Then he opened the door of his bedchamber and walked into the next room. Tinkerbelle sat up, stretched and then, with a look of mild irritation, set off behind him. The King walked from the next room into the next and then from the next into the next and then… and so on. The castle was dark and empty apart from the occasional guard who jumped to his feet and looked alarmed as the King strode past him followed by Tinkerbelle, her tail held high. On and on and round and round walked the King, all the time muttering to himself, "Oh dear, oh dear" and "What can this be? What can this be?" Tinkerbelle kept him company, but said nothing.

And then, walking through the library, he came upon an Old Man he had never seen before. The Old Man was sitting in one of the great armchairs of the library and because, the chair was big and he was small, it would have been possible to walk by without noticing him at all. Except that he wore a bright yellow cap with a green tassel and was eating a large apple rather noisily.

Perhaps it was because the King was tired of walking, or perhaps it was the yellow cap with the green tassel, or perhaps it was the noise of the apple being eaten – whatever the reason was – the King stopped and sat down in another of the armchairs, whilst Tinkerbelle did the same, thinking to herself, "Well at least we have stopped walking."

All of this seemed to have no effect on the Old Man, who continued eating his apple, apparently unaware of the King.

"Excuse me," said the King, leaning towards the Old Man, "excuse me, but it is not often that I come across a man with a yellow cap and a green tassel eating an apple so noisily in my library."

"Oh, this is your library is it?" said the Old Man.

"Yes," said the King.

"And are these your armchairs?"

"Yes."

"Then I must suppose this is also your apple. And very good it is too." And with that the Old Man took his last bite and, tossing the core in the direction of the fireplace, wiped his hands and his beard with a large pink and white spotted handkerchief pulled from inside the sleeve of his coat. Then he belched. "That's better," said the Old Man.

The King was so overcome by all of this that he could not move, but sat there and stared at the Old Man, captivated by his performance.

"It's rude to stare," said the Old Man.

"It's rude to sit in someone else's chair, in someone else's library, eating someone else's apple," replied the King.

"Not at all," said the old Man. "I was waiting for you."

"Waiting for me!" exclaimed the King, now beginning to feel that this was all completely out of order. "Why would you be waiting for me?"

"Well," said the Old Man, "I was waiting for you because you are frightened, and I thought you would like some company."

"Frightened," said the King. "Frightened, what makes you think I am frightened?"

"Well, you look frightened," said the Old Man.

And at that moment Tinkerbelle got up from her chair and jumped into the Old Man's lap. He stroked her.

Tinkerbelle began to purr and the Old Man closed his eyes as if he were going to have a nap.

"Just a moment," said the King. "It's all very well for you to sit there stroking my cat and having a nap, but I should point out that it is I who is the King not you. I may stroke my cat and I may have a nap whenever I please, but that is because I am the King, whereas nobody knows who you are at all."

"I do," said Tinkerbelle to herself, but no one heard her since no one ever listens to a cat.

"Well that may be so", said the Old Man. "That may well be so. Indeed, it is most certainly so. But then you are afraid and I am not."

"There you go again," said the King, his voice now rising in what might have been thought to be anxiety. "You have no reason to suppose that I am frightened."

The Old Man said nothing.

"I may occasionally be a little worried," continued the King. "I may even from time to time, but not very often, be more than a little worried."

The Old Man said nothing.

"All right, "said the King, I will agree that there have been just one or two moments when I have been just the tiniest bit frightened."

"Like tonight," said the Old Man opening his eyes and looking at the King.

"Well yes," said the King. "As you have mentioned it, I will say that this evening in bed, I was rather taken by what I suppose might be called being frightened."

"There we are," said the old Man, "that was not all that difficult was it?"

"What do you mean," said the King. "What do mean it wasn't difficult?"

"Well," said the Old Man, closing his eyes again, "it wasn't difficult to admit that you were frightened."

"Oh, get on with it," thought Tinkerbelle, but she kept the thought to herself.

Of course the King knew that he was frightened, but he had not really wanted to admit it – didn't want to let it in, let the fear creep in and find its way into his head, into his stomach and, of course, into his heart. But there it was.

"And can you tell me," said the Old Man, "what it is that you are frightened about?"

"Oh, nothing really," said the King. "Nothing much."

That's very odd," said the Old Man. "I once knew a King who was frightened by a fierce band of brigands that was encamped around his castle. And I came across another that was frightened about the violent storms that poured rain upon him, flooding his fields and gutters. I even once met a King who was frightened of caterpillars and spiders. But I have never before met a King who was frightened by nothing at all."

"And not very likely to do so," thought Tinkerbelle. But she kept the thought to herself since no one ever listens to a cat.

"Well," said the King, not wishing to appear foolish, "there is something that frightens me."

"And what is that?" said the Old Man. Or he would have said that had not, at that moment, four of the King's guards rushed into the room and grabbed him by his collar.

"What on earth are you doing," said the King jumping from his chair. "Let him go! Let him go!"

"Well, Sir," said the Chief Guard, dropping the Old Man back into the armchair, "its just that we saw you stride past, and then we saw Tinkerbelle following you with her tail in the air, and then we saw this Old Man sitting in your library with a yellow cap and a green tassel, and he looked very dangerous and very threatening."

"Dangerous! Threatening!" shouted the King. "How can an Old Man with a yellow cap and a green tassel be dangerous and threatening?"

"Well, Sir," said the Chief Guard, now fearful that he had brought displeasure upon himself. "You never know. You just never know." And with that, he and the other guards began to back out of the library, bowing low, first to the King, then to Tinkerbelle and then, somewhat reluctantly, to the Old Man.

"Come back!" commanded the King. "Since you are here you might as well do something useful. Go at once to the kitchen, make up a jug of hot chocolate and bring it here with two cups, a saucer for Tinkerbelle and a plate of biscuits."

And so they did. And before long, the King, Tinkerbelle and the Old Man were sitting together enjoying the hot drink and the biscuits.

As a warm peacefulness spread amongst them, both the King and the Old Man stretched out their legs so that they rested on the low table between them, and Tinkerbelle, not to be left out, licked the last drops of chocolate from her saucer and stretched out in her own chair, leaning against one of the cushions that had been placed upon it.

"So what is it, my dear King," said the Old Man. "What is it that frightens you?"

The King was silent for a moment, finding the courage to say what he had known from the very first moment that he had felt the fear creep into his bones. One by one, as the warmth of the hot chocolate found its way into his stomach, the words came to him.

"I fear," he said. "I fear dying," he said. "I fear dying alone," he said. And then it all tumbled out. "I fear, being ill and dying alone."

The Old Man said nothing, but nibbled on his biscuit.

Tinkerbelle smiled to herself.

Oddly, once he had said it, once he had admitted it, once, sitting there with the Old Man he had brought it into full view, the King somehow knew that the fear was less than he had thought. Out in the open, no longer hidden but sitting there in front of him, the fear had shrivelled up. And somewhat to his astonishment, he heard himself say, "But of course, if I had to, if that is what happened, I could die by myself. I could do that. I don't want to, but if I had to, I could."

The Old Man said nothing but brushed the crumbs from his coat onto the floor of the library. And Tinkerbelle began to purr.

There was a long silence and then the King stood up and picking up the tray of the now empty cups and the saucer, with the plate upon which the biscuits had once been, carried it to a table near the door of the library.

"You see," he said, turning around and addressing his remark to the Old Man, "you see…" But the Old Man was not there. The chair in which he had been sitting was empty. Only Tinkerbelle remained, now licking her paws and washing behind her ears.

"Oh," said the King, "he seems to have gone."

"And what would you expect?" said Tinkerbelle. But no one ever listens to a cat.

The King picked her up and walked back to his bedchamber. She returned to her basket on the blanket box, and the King took off his dressing gown and slippers and, getting into his bed, pulled his duvet around himself, turned on his side and went to sleep. He slept well whilst Tinkerbelle quietly left her basket and found her way through an open window into the garden for her nightly prowl.

Nothing was ever quite the same again.

On the morning of the next day, the King woke to find all sorts of people in the rooms of his castle – his housekeeper had made his breakfast, his cleaner was cleaning, his gardener was gardening, the man who had come to service the Aga and the man who had come to look at the leak in his roof were both busily working away. Tinkerbelle had returned to the castle and had found a sunny spot on a sofa in the Garden

Room where she was seemingly asleep. And, as if for the first time, the King realised that, of course, he did not live by himself at all. His daughter rang him to say hello and his son sent a note confirming his visit later that week.

Later that afternoon, walking in the garden of his castle and talking to his gardener about some new lavender plants that were being put into large pots, the King thought he caught sight of someone wearing a yellow cap with a green tassel disappearing into one of the shrubberies. But when he looked again there was no one there, and he was not sure if he had seen anyone at all. Anyway it made him smile.

And so he walked back into his castle and asked for his tea to be brought to him in the Garden Room where, finding an armchair next to the sofa upon which Tinkerbelle appeared to be sleeping and purring at one and the same time, he took a nap.

"I wonder," thought Tinkerbelle to herself, "I wonder whether he caught site of the Old Man in the shrubbery." But no one ever listens to a cat.

FINDING ELSEWHERE

LUCY AND THE EYE OF THE STORM

One morning Lucy sat in her kitchen holding a cup of tea in her hands. Both of her teenage children had recently left home, but whilst she was feeling sad and a bit lonely she also felt curious. And so there she was, sitting in her kitchen and wondering what to do next or rather what might happen.

Later that day, Lucy was talking about this to her friend Mary whilst they stood in a queue at the Co-op. Such conversations can hardly be private, and perhaps they are not meant to be. And so it was that a comfortable looking woman who was standing in front of them, said: "Excuse me for butting in, but perhaps you should go and see the Old Man who lives across the meadows some way away from the town. He is known to be wise, or so I have been told, and perhaps he would be able to help you."

Going to talk to old men was not something that Lucy had ever thought of doing, especially if they lived across meadows far from the town.

"Do you really think he could help me?" she asked.

"Well unless you try you will never find out," said the comfortable looking woman, "and anyway I must be off. I only popped in for a bag of almonds." And that was that.

When she arrived home and was settling down to her lunch – Ryvita, avocado and pear – Lucy began to wonder whether she might, perhaps, seek out the Old Man. "After all," she thought, "what have I to lose, and the adventure might be just what I need."

The next morning, once again standing in the queue in the Co-op, which must surely be the source of all useful information, she began to make enquiries about directions and distances. Quite a lot of people had heard about the Old Man and each of them had something to say. And so it was that a few days later, as Summer gave way to Autumn, Lucy set out, placing in her bag a bottle of water, a packet of nuts and raisins, and a pad and pencil, with which she supposed she would write down the advice she would be given.

She left the town and set off along the path that she had been told would lead her to the Old Man's cottage. She had pulled her hair back into a ponytail, set beneath a soft beret of plum red. Her woollen coat was long and warm, gathered at her waist by a belt braided in many colours. She walked with a firm stride, but despite her red beret she felt very uneasy.

At first, the path seemed quite ordinary and well

trodden, but as she left the town behind her it became more difficult to follow, becoming narrower and in part overgrown. After some while, tired by the walking and having to push back the brambles that now crossed the path, Lucy stopped and sat upon a fallen tree, opening her bag, taking a sip of her water and eating some of her nuts and raisins. Looking back, the town had now disappeared from view and all around her Lucy could see only meadows and hedgerows, some with large trees now showing their Autumn colours. There was no sense of danger and yet, as the sun passed behind clouds, Lucy felt a chill reaching into her, working its way beneath her coat.

For a moment, she thought that she should, perhaps, turn back and return home. But at that very moment, the sun reappeared from behind the clouds, and as she felt its warmth her courage returned. She reached up to the tie that held her hair and let it fall to her shoulders.

"That's better," said a voice, but when she looked around she could see no one other than a rather dishevelled sparrow waiting to pick up the crumbs of her food.

"That's odd," she thought, and she put away her water bottle and after throwing down some nuts onto the ground, put her bag over her shoulder and set off once more.

Now the path was clear, and in the distance she saw smoke rising from the chimney of what she supposed must be the Old Man's cottage. The smoke rose in a spiral turning and spreading up and away.

As she walked through the meadow and along the hedgerows, Lucy felt a strange mixture of lightness and intensity in her footsteps. All around her there was a chatter of birdsong and what seemed to be the murmuring of a fresh and gentle breeze. Stopping for a moment, she thought once more that she could hear voices. But looking around she could not see anyone there. She listened again, and then it was that she realised that the voices were coming from the hedgerow. It was as if the trees in the hedgerow were talking to each other. Earlier that day, this would have been absurd, but now, in the magic of the meadow, it seemed not surprising at all. Lucy was entering another world.

It was not long before she found herself at the gate of the Old Man's garden. It had rather a beautiful wooden gate, carved with flowers, fruit and vegetables and set within a roofed archway. Opening the gate, Lucy walked up the path that led to the cottage amidst beds of late flowering hydrangeas, now deep red in colour, the pink and white flowers of cosmos and the purple flowers of verbena. She knocked on the door, but there was no reply. She knocked again. No reply.

It was then that she saw the Old Man walking through an adjoining meadow, picking up things from the ground and placing them in a large wicker basket that he was carrying. As she walked towards him, the Old Man turned and waved as if he had been expecting her to arrive at that very moment. Not wishing to intrude, Lucy waited for the Old Man to return to his cottage, his basket now full of what looked like gnarled truffles.

"I don't know," he said as he came into his garden, "I don't know. Each day there seem to be more and more of these, and I am expected to pick them up and make them better. Why can't people do this themselves? Why should I have to do it for them?"

Lucy had no idea what he was talking about.

"It's all the grudges," said the Old Man. "I have to pick them up and take them in, and then I have to place them in my steamer, clean them up, mash them into tiny pieces and then give them to the mice and squirrels to return to the town as compost. They leave them in gardens and at the foot of trees, you know. All very nutritious."

And with that, and beckoning to Lucy to follow him, he carried his basket into his cottage and poured the grudges into a large pot of boiling water standing on his stove. Soon the steam had engulfed them all.

"Well," said the Old Man, "we can leave them there for a while. Would you like some tea? Yes of course you would. And some cake?"

And with that kettles, tins and teapots were put to work until cups of tea and slices of a cake were arranged on a large tray, which the Old Man carried from the kitchen into his sitting room. Having taken off her beret and coat and laid them on a chair, Lucy picked up her bag and followed him. Soon she was sitting on a deep and soft sofa arrayed with many cushions and blankets, whilst the Old Man sat in his favourite armchair and, having poured the tea and pushed the slices of cake towards her, placed his feet on the low table between them, his hands clasped together upon his round and generous stomach.

As she drank her tea, Lucy looked around the Old Man's room. As she had expected, there were a great many books. But then she noticed there were also a great many boxes and jars, each of which was labelled. Somewhat to her surprise she found that the labels did not say things such as 'Paper Clips' or 'Envelopes' or even 'Toffees' or 'Liquorice Allsorts'. They said things like 'The Eye of the Storm', 'The Light of the Moon', 'The Turn of the Wave' and 'The Wetness of Dew'.

Noticing her surprise, the Old Man said, "I suppose you have never seen such things before?"

"No, I have not," she replied.

"Well how do you think they come about?" he said. "Surely you don't think they arise out of nothing?"

"No, I suppose not," she said, noticing more labels such as 'The Coldness of Ice', 'The Heat of the Flame', 'The Whiff of Hypocrisy' and 'The Falling of the Apple'.

The Old Man reached up and took down from its shelf the box marked 'The Eye of the Storm'. Opening the lid, he took out a small flat disk, dark in colour. As he held out his hand to show it to her, Lucy could see that the disk was still and calm whilst at its edge was a mist moving anti-clockwise, round and round in a circle. And when she placed her finger on the disk, she found it had no substance at all. Her finger passed right through and touched the Old Man's hand.

Putting the disk back in its box and placing the box back on its shelf, as if this were nothing strange at all, the Old Man dusted crumbs of cake from his stomach and sitting back in his armchair closed his eyes.

"Well," said Lucy wanting to turn the conversation away from boxes and jars and towards the purpose of her visit, "this is all very well but…"

"But," interrupted the Old Man, his eyes still closed, "but I cannot answer your question."

"But I haven't asked it yet," she said somewhat put out by his reply. "And if I haven't asked it, how do you know what it was I was going to ask?"

"I didn't say I knew what you were going to ask," said the Old Man. "I simply said that I could not give you an answer."

"But what does that mean?" asked Lucy, now feeling rather more than a little confused.

"What is it that you do not understand?" he replied now sitting up and looking straight into Lucy's eyes. "Surely it is quite straight forward. I simply said that I can't answer your question. I cannot answer your question. If it were my question, I could probably answer it, but since it is yours I can't."

And with that he got up from his chair, picked up the tea tray and set off for his kitchen where, almost at once, there could be heard the sounds of water running into a sink and then plates and cups evidently being washed.

Lucy waited for a moment gathering her thoughts, not at all understanding what had happened. She stood up, looked again at the many boxes and jars on the shelves of the Old Man's room, and walked into the kitchen.

There was no sign of the Old Man in the kitchen. In fact there was no sign of the Old Man anywhere. And so, somewhat disappointed, Lucy took up her bag, put on her beret and coat, and walked out of the cottage, down the path and through the gate. Turning back, she caught sight of the Old Man in the meadow behind the cottage, once again bent down and picking up what she now knew were grudges. She waved, but he did not see her, or so it seemed.

Lucy made her way back to the town, past the gossiping hedgerow, along which a Barn Owl now hunted, gliding and swooping in the dusk. She walked across the meadows, past the fallen tree and the brambles, along the well trodden path until, as the darkness of the evening began to creep in, she was on the edge of the town and then home. When she emptied her bag and looked at her notepad, she noticed that she had written nothing upon it.

In the days that followed, Lucy wondered what had happened at the Old Man's Cottage and, indeed, whether it had happened at all. She thought much about The Eye of the Storm, The Light of the Moon, the Turn of the Wave and The Wetness of Dew. And she thought a bit about The Coldness of Ice, The Heat of the Flame, The Whiff of Hypocrisy and The Falling of the Apple. She could make nothing of it, but then one moonlit night, sitting in her garden, she did hold moonlight in her hand, and one morning she touched with her finger the wetness of the dew, noticing the multitude of gossamer spider webs on a patch of grass.

Indeed, she found she was spending more and more time in her garden. Until the children had left home, the garden had simply been a place that everyone ran around in or sometimes left bikes there or lay out on rugs to sunbathe. But now, it had become quieter and often a remarkable stillness seemed to settle upon it. One day, in the middle of the morning, sitting on a chair she had taken from the kitchen and drinking a second cup of tea, Lucy began to look at her garden as if for the first time. She looked and she looked and, in the quietness, she thought for a moment that she heard chattering voices and birdsong.

It was then that she decided to make herself a garden. She hurried indoors and found a few scraps of paper and a pencil and began to make some notes. She drew out possible flowerbeds and a place for an apple tree, and she began to list the plants she felt might suit the garden, with its patches of sunlight and shade. And as if she had suddenly remembered something, she marked a place for the making of compost. She spent the whole day drawing her plans and then altering them and starting again, not really knowing what it was that she would do.

Then she went to bed and slept.

The next morning, when she came into her kitchen to make breakfast, Lucy found on the table a parcel wrapped in scraps of paper and tied with string. Unwrapping it, she found inside a large and somewhat battered book. Its title was *An Old Man's Garden Book.*

"So perhaps it did happen after all," she thought, "perhaps it did happen." And opening the book she found page upon page of pictures and information and a bookmark, which was set at a page titled 'What and When to Plant'.

"This is exactly what I need," said Lucy and, not for a moment wondering how the book had come to be on her table, she began her work. Soon, her garden plan was marked with more notes and with dates for planting.

To begin with she decided that she would dig out her beds, drawing them onto the ground with trickles of white flour. Then, consulting the *Garden Book* she dug deeply. As she had no compost of her own, she dug in sacks of compost bought from the Garden Centre she had found quite nearby, and her car soon began to look like a garden shed.

She planned her planting for the following Spring, but wanting to get ahead with the apple trees, she attended a number of apple tastings before selecting, purchasing and planting bare root stocks of Bramley Seedling and Cox's Orange Pippin. In late November, she planted them, securing each with a stout wooden stake. Fortunately, there were many different apple trees in the gardens nearby and, as it happened, both trees thrived.

According to the *Garden Book* it was rather late to plant daffodil and narcissus bulbs, but she decided to try anyway, scattering the bulbs towards the end of her garden, and then she planted several pots of tulip bulbs, gathering them together in a sunny spot close to her kitchen door.

Throughout the Winter, as the magic of the dark time took place within the earth, her plans, too, took shape and for Christmas Lucy bought herself a small greenhouse in which, in early February, after the feast of Imbolc, she began to plant her seeds. First she planted the seeds of cosmos, delphiniums and lupins. Then, in long pots, she planted sweet peas. She also purchased her seed potatoes, Charlottes, setting them out to chit in egg boxes on a sunny windowsill in her kitchen, and turning them week by week to nourish the shoots when they came.

Later in the Spring, as the bulbs came through, Lucy was able to plant out all the plants that she had grown and cared for in her greenhouse, providing a tower made of willow for the sweet peas. She began her first sowing of salad crops: lettuce, spinach, beetroot and the first sowing of her broad beans. She also bought a very large pot into which she planted herbs: thyme, marjoram and basil, with a separate pot for mint.

Later she planted climbing roses and a honeysuckle, and by the Summer time, Lucy's garden was in full flower, attracting first bumble bees and honey bees and then later butterflies, drawn to a large buddleia in her neighbour's garden. Now that her ears had become attuned, there were times when the noise in the garden, as each plant spoke to its neighbour or called across the flowerbed to an old friend, was cacophonous. But at other times the stillness and the silence were so deep Lucy thought she might drown. She had become a part of the garden. It was the place in which she had to be.

And so it went on. That Autumn she planted her own buddleia bush and then lavender in large glazed clay pots.

Not surprisingly, with all of this happening, Lucy spent much of her time, in fact most of her time, in her garden. Often quite unaware of what was happening elsewhere. She no longer read the newspaper or listened to the news. She did not have time to do so, and anyway she no longer felt the need. Her children phoned from time to time, but they did not visit very often. Their lives were busy and distant. Oddly, Lucy hardly noticed. She was always pleased to hear from them and even to see them for short visits, but there was always something to do in the garden. And there were new friends, people she met at the Garden Centre who wanted to see how her garden was doing and who invited her to visit them, too. Or it was neighbours who stopped for a chat as they were walking by and she was digging or planting or pruning.

She felt the 'turn of the season', 'the warmth of the sun' and 'the coldness of frost'; and she saw 'the budding of the blossom', 'the unfurling of the leaves' and 'the falling of the apples'. And when she did so, she remembered the Old Man's boxes and jars and knew from whence these things had come.

And then one morning looking out of her kitchen window at her garden and wondering what needed to be done that day, she saw a line of mice and two squirrels, each one carrying a small bag of what seemed to be compost and scattering it around her plants and around the trunks of her apple trees.

Lucy laughed and pulling her hair back into a ponytail she put on her plum red beret and her coat, long and warm and gathered at her waist by a belt braided with many colours. It was then that she found in her coat pocket a scrap of paper upon which was written:

'Love shapes all and will shape you when you surrender.'

LUCY AND THE EYE OF THE STORM

ENDINGS

FINDING ELSEWHERE

FINDING ELSEWHERE

Love is most nearly itself
When here and now cease to matter.
Old men ought to be explorers
Here or there does not matter
We must be still and still moving
Into another intensity
For a further union, a deeper communion
Through the dark cold and the empty desolation,
The wave cry, the wind cry, the vast waters
Of the petrel and the porpoise. In my end is
my beginning.

   T. S. Eliot, *Four Quartets, East Coker, Part V*

The Old Man knelt in the meadow, trying to shift the heavy load on his back. He struggled, but it would not move. He was tired, deeply tired – tiredness that came from a long time. And then the struggle ended. The Old Man dropped his arms and rested his hands upon the ground. There was no more he could do.

The load slipped. He was free.

After a while, he looked up and saw before him a path. It ran across the meadow and towards a wood. The path was clear and the ground was dry. It had been worn away by the feet of all those who had passed this way before him. The meadow was strewn with wildflowers, yellow rattle, canterbury pink, white daisy and cowslip. He took a deep breath and let the tears flow from his eyes. He knew where he was and where the path would take him. He lay down in the sweet meadow.

He lay there, and for a day and a night he slept. He needed to rest. He was about to begin a journey and in his linen bag was just enough to take him there, a bottle of water and a sandwich.

After a while, when the sun had dried the meadow and when the damselflies had begun their work, the Old Man sat up and took a sip of water. So this was it. For some time, he had known that he would find himself here. And now he was.

"Odd," he thought, "very odd."

Taking his stick and putting on his straw hat, he pulled himself up and, putting the linen bag over his head and across his chest, he began to walk. For several days he walked towards the wood, and each morning he thought he would reach it by eventide, but he didn't. And so, each night he slept and each morning when he awoke the wood seemed just as far away as it had the day before. But the meadow was sweet, the grass high and the flowers full of bees, and this continued day after day until he no longer sought the wood but gave himself to the walking.

No-one knows how long he walked through the meadow. Some say a few days, some a few years. But each morning he found his water bottle full and a freshly made sandwich in his bag, sometimes cheese and pickle, sometimes honey and banana and some-times cherries and marmalade. As the days went by, the walking pleased him – and the tall grass, the damselflies and the bees. Whereas, at first, he had felt weary and sometimes breathless, the walking seemed to become easier and a stillness and feeling of well-being overcame him. Each night as he lay down to sleep beneath the stars, his head resting on his linen bag, he lay his stick across the path to mark his place. All was quiet and peaceful.

Then one morning, when he woke the stillness and the quietness were so deep he could hardly breathe. A light mist had settled over the meadow. Nothing moved. Opening his eyes, he saw, further along the path, a large hare sitting and looking towards him, its ears upright and alert. And there, perched upon his hat which lay upon the ground, was a small bird. It was not at all colourful, its back a dull brown and its breast grey, but its eyes were bright with a circle of yellow around each one and its beak was thin and delicate. Suddenly, the bird was in full trill, its head uplifted and its beak open wide, a small tongue causing the sound to ripple.

At once, the Old Man knew that the hare and the bird were there to guide him, messengers from another world. He stood up, drank from his water bottle and took a bite of his sandwich – cherries and marmalade.

The bird fluttered about him, darting backwards and forwards until the Old Man began to follow the direction of the hare, who bounded along the path. And this time, as he walked towards it, the wood came closer and closer until the Old Man found himself at its edge.

The wood was dark and cool, but the path was there and the Old Man followed it. At first he could not see where it was going, but after a while he could see an opening of light, with the hare sitting in the middle of the path and the bird flying to and fro.

"So this is it," said the Old Man to himself, and for a moment he looked back along the path he had trodden, fearing he would never come this way again. His old world lay back along the track in the meadow. His new world lay before him, although, at that time, he could have had no idea what it would be and what challenges it would bring. If he had known, he might not have continued.

When the Old Man came to the furthermost edge of the wood he had expected to find another fine meadow, perhaps with flowers even more beautiful than before. But much to his surprise it was not so. There was a meadow, but it was scrubby and within a short distance there stood what seemed to be a town. Certainly there were a large number of rather drab looking houses and people scurrying to and fro. And then, as he came nearer, he saw a great many horse-drawn carts and handcarts piled with what looked like old rags, some steaming and others dank and limp. These carts seemed to be going between the houses, emptying their contents and then moving off into the countryside beyond the town.

The sky was now somewhat overcast, but peppered with gaps in the cloud where the sun shone through with intense brightness, lighting up the gardens of each of the houses. In fact, the clouds seemed to rise up from the houses rather than cover them from above. And as he came closer he could see that those driving the carts or pushing them along were not at all drab. Indeed, their clothes were of the most beautiful colours, some made of patchwork and others embroidered with patterns of flowers, birds, animals and sometimes butterflies. Their hair was long and of all colours, some white, some fair, some dark black and others brown or auburn flecked with light.

"How strange," thought the Old Man.

The hare and the bird had gone on before him and now seemed to be taking him to one of the houses at the edge of the town where, as it did everywhere else in the town, the sun shone into a garden, this one surrounded by a hawthorn and beech hedge amongst which ran a briar rose. He followed.

As he came to the house, the Old Man began to feel uneasy. This was not at all what he had expected to find. He had somehow supposed that in this Otherworld all would be light, with widespread countryside and only a few houses here and there. But then he thought to himself, how could this really be. The world he had left behind was dark and over-crowded. Nearly everyone there lived in a city and only very few people lived in the countryside remote from a town. Why should this world be so different?

The hare sat at the front door and the bird sat on the windowsill. Slowly the Old Man walked up to the door of the house and knocked. There was no reply, but as he knocked the door opened into a hallway. He stepped inside and all was dark, the windows shuttered. For a moment the Old Man waited, unsure as to what was expected of him. But then he opened the shutters and let in the light.

The house was almost bare, except for a few pieces of furniture and one or two rugs on the floor. He went from room to room, opening the shutters as he went, his heart pounding and his mood falling. Was this what he had hoped for? No it was not, and he now began to wish he had not sought this Otherworld, but had stayed behind.

At last, he walked though into a kitchen. Opening the shutters and letting in the sunlight, he found a warm range and a plain wooden table with four chairs around it. There was a larder and cupboards with cups and saucers and plates. A bread bin sat on the sideboard and when he lifted the lid there was the comforting smell of newly baked bread. The kettle

on the range was coming to the boil and a tin marked
'Tea' sat beside it.

Feeling a little better, the Old Man walked through
the kitchen towards a pair of doors that led into the
garden. Before he reached them they opened and
there, full of sunlight, was the most beautiful cottage
garden he had ever seen – hollyhocks and geraniums,
cosmos and roses and an apple tree. The garden was
full of birdsong and he thought he saw the small dull
brown bird in one of the bushes. The hare seemed
to have had gone.

"So," he thought to himself, "here is something
unexpected and difficult to understand. Darkness
and sunlight, sorrow and delight."

But that was just the beginning.

That night, after darkness had come upon the house
and the moon was high, the Old Man made himself
some supper, pouring hot water from the kettle into a
small brown pot into which he had put a spoon of the
tea from the tin, and eating the last of his sandwiches
– honey and banana. Then, yawning and rubbing
his head, he made his way upstairs to find a place to
sleep. The first room he found was just right. It had
in it a large bed with fresh sheets, a most beautiful
quilt and soft pillows. There was a cupboard which,
much to his surprise, had some of his clothes in it, and
drawers where he found shirts and pants and vests.
Tucked beneath a chair, he even found a pair of his
tapestry slippers. A door led to a bathroom where
he discovered his toothpaste and even the particular

kind of soap he liked to use.

Perhaps he should have stopped there, but his curiosity got the better of him. Leaving his bedroom behind he began to explore the rest of the rooms.

The first door he tried was locked and the next so stuck that he could not open it. Perhaps he should have seen this as a warning, but he did not. He persisted. And the next door opened.

At first he could see nothing. It was dark, very dark and there seemed to be something piled up in the middle of the room. The Old Man edged his way around the walls until he came to a window. He tried to open the shutters but they were very stiff. He tried again and one of them moved just enough to let in the moonlight. The light fell across the room and onto what was in the middle – a pile of dark and flapping rags, moving to some inner rhythm up and down and round and round. The air, vile and stale, choked him so that he ran from the room and shut the door, leaning against the wall of the corridor and gasping for breath.

Slowly he made his way along the corridor to the sanctuary of his own bedroom, closed the door behind him, locked it and fell upon the bed. He slept.

The next morning, when the Old Man woke, he lay for a while wondering where he was and why it was that he was lying on this large bed fully clothed. Then he remembered and a cold chill ran all over him. He covered himself in the quilt and curled himself into a ball, wishing he had stayed at home and not set off on this adventure.

But then the shutter on one of the bedroom windows swung open and there was the small bird singing full trill. Fluttering to and fro, she fussed around him until, in order to make her stop, he got up, took off his clothes and went into the bathroom, where he washed himself from top to toe. After this he felt much better and dressed himself in fresh clothes.

As he was putting on his shoes, he heard a noise coming from downstairs. It sounded very much like someone making breakfast. The Old Man opened his door a little and, yes, there was definitely the smell of toast. Encouraged, he made his way down the stairs and into the kitchen, where he found a comfortable looking woman in a flowery dress and a colourful pinafore making tea. She was obviously someone's mother.

"Good morning," she said. "I am your Housekeeper and I am glad you are up as you have a lot of work to do today and lying about in bed will not get it done. Marmalade with your toast, or would you like honey?"

"Marmalade, please," said the Old Man, as if nothing strange had happened at all.

And so he sat at the table and had his breakfast, whilst his Housekeeper made tea and then began washing the kitchen floor with a large bucket of soapy water and a mop. The Old Man lifted his feet and held onto the table so that she could wash all around him and then pour the soapy water down the sink.

"Now," said the Housekeeper, "very soon your helpers will be here and you will have to start your work."

"My work?" said the Old Man. "And what is my work?"

"Laundry," said the Housekeeper wiping her hands on her pinafore. "Laundry, cutting and sewing. This house is not just for you to lie around in or sit having cups of tea. It is a laundry and a workshop. All the houses in this town are the same. Our work is to wash and dry all those rags you saw last night; to refresh them and then to cut them into very small pieces of colour and send them back."

"Send them back?" asked the Old Man. "Send them back where?"

"Send them back to your world," replied the Housekeeper. "How else do you think there would be colour there?"

The Old Man's head was spinning as he tried to make sense of what his Housekeeper was saying.

"You will have to explain this to me a bit more," he said. "At the moment I have no idea what you are talking about."

"Right," she said, "let's start at the beginning. You have seen the cartloads of drab and smelly rags in this town and you have already found the room upstairs which is full of them?"

"Yes," said the Old Man.

"Well," continued the Housekeeper, now sitting opposite him at the table and taking sips from a large and flowery mug of tea, "all the sorrow and suffering of your world finds its way here in the form of these rags, which are then brought to the houses to be laundered. This town is just one of many, but when we receive the rags we wash them and hang them on washing lines in the sunshine of the garden. You will have noticed that the gardens are always full of sunlight?"

"Yes," said the Old Man.

Well," she continued, "when the rags are dry and their colour has been restored, we cut them into small pieces, which are then carried back into your world in all sorts of ways. The birds carry them, the bees and damselflies carry them and they are carried in the water of streams and rivers. Some are taken underground by ants and other insects, and some are pushed into rocks and stones. In all these ways your world becomes colourful. And how do you think the sky is kept so blue? Have you any idea how many small patches of blue are sown together to do that; and have you ever thought how much work it takes to repair the sky when it wears through...?"

"Of course you haven't," she continued, her voice now touched with irritation. "You and your kind just assume that the beauty of the flowers in your garden and the wings of butterflies and dragonflies happen by chance. Well, you are wrong. It takes a lot of work – tiring and meticulous work. And as it happens, we in this world are getting a bit fed up with the way in which you and your people treat your world, so indifferent as you are to its beauty and so careless as you are of its wonder. Indeed, we are becoming increasingly concerned that we may not be able to keep up with the piles of ragged sorrows and sufferings you send to us. We are being overwhelmed by your carelessness and your sorrow. Why can't you take more responsibility for this yourselves? Have you ever thought what will happen if we are overwhelmed? Of course you haven't, because you are selfish and stupid!"

And with this, she stood up and walked off, leaving the Old Man gasping at the onslaught.

A little later, others began to arrive, immediately setting about their work, collecting the dingy rags from the upper room and taking them out in baskets to the washroom attached to the house. Then after much sloshing and soaping and rinsing and wringing, the rags were taken into the garden and pegged to line upon line, each one propped up by a long wooden pole until, in the rays of the sun they were dry and restored to colour. As soon as this had happened, other people collected the colourful rags together and took them to the workroom alongside the laundry where they were cut and sown. Some were sown together as patchwork quilts and others woven together as rugs, but most were placed into tiny baskets and placed on racks in the garden. During the rest of that day, flocks of birds and swarms of insects came into the garden picking up the tiny baskets and setting off to deliver their colours to every corner of the Old Man's world, to the highest and the lowest parts and from those furthest East and those furthest West. Some were carried off and floated into the streams and rivers that ran back into this world, glistening the scales of fish and resting in the pebbles and stones.

So taken with all this work was the old Man that he was unaware of the passing of the day, but then, at about four o'clock in the afternoon, the Housekeeper arrived with trays of tea and cakes and everyone stopped for a while and rested. The Old Man took his mug of tea and sat beside the Housekeeper and asked her a question.

"If the colours of my world come from the trans-formation of sorrows and sadness, what happens to the groans of pain and what happens to the weeping of tears?"

"I am surprised you know so little," she replied. "As you can imagine all of these come here as well. Where else could they go? And then they are caught in butterfly nets and jam jars. The groans of pain are transformed into birdsong and the murmuring of the wind, and the tears are poured back into the rivers and streams where, in the swirling of the waters, they are refreshed and restored."

"Anyway," she went on, "I have no time to sit here and tell you things you should already know. I am making apple crumble and custard for supper."

For many days and weeks, or was it months and years, the Old Man remained in the Otherworld until his skill in all the processes of healing and transformation became so well known that visitors from other towns would sometimes call by to talk to him and watch him at work. He seemed to be entirely at home.

Then, as the days or years passed by, he began to notice that from time to time one or two of the town's people could be seen setting off along the track he had followed as if they were walking back towards the wood. So one morning, as he sat at the table, his hands holding his mug of tea, he asked the Housekeeper what they were doing.

"From time to time," she said, "some of the town's people decide they want to go back to your world. They discover that they have not really finished their time there, or they are called back by someone who needs them and wonders where they are. And so, they pack a bag with one of our quilts or one of our rugs and they go back. And when they arrive they find that it is as if they had only been gone for an hour or so, as if they had just returned from a short walk."

Over the next several days, the Old Man found himself pondering on this. And as the days went by, the thoughts would not go away. Indeed, they grew stronger and stronger until one evening, at supper time, when his Housekeeper was serving up poached eggs on toast, he had to say it.

"I want to go back," he said. "I have not finished my work and now I need to tell my people that we must take more responsibility for the delights of our world: the colours of the plants and of the birds and insects and the colours in the rocks and grains of sand; the murmuring of the wind and the birdsong; the clear running streams and the blueness of the sky. I must go back."

"I know," said the Housekeeper, and when you go to bed tonight you will see that I have already packed you a bag with a colourful quilt and a rug. And tomorrow I will give you some sandwiches and a bottle of water for your journey."

"Can I have banana and honey?" asked the Old Man.

"Of course you can," she replied.

The next morning, the Old Man woke early and washed and dressed, finding beside his bed the bag that his Housekeeper had prepared for him – a quilt, a rug and bottle of water, two banana and honey sandwiches and a clean pair of pants, just in case. Downstairs he could hear her preparing breakfast and soon he was there, sitting at the table and holding his mug of tea, whilst his Housekeeper prepared the bucket of soapy water to clean the kitchen floor. He lifted his feet and held onto the table so that she could clean around him and then with a great deal of sloshing, pour the dirty water down the sink.

"All is well," he thought to himself.

He wanted to say his thanks to her for all she had done for him, but she would have none of it and shushed him out of the front door, from where he could see the track leading to the wood.

The Old Man picked up his bag put on his hat and said, "Good bye."

And then, just as he was about to set off, he turned to the Housekeeper and said, "Tell me, my dear Housekeeper, where is this Otherworld and how shall I ever find it again?"

"It is wherever you are," she replied. "It is always and everywhere. And you will find it whenever you turn towards it and start to walk along the path."

"Keep my room ready for me," said the Old Man.

"I will," she replied.

And there further down the track the Old Man could see the hare and little brown bird waiting for him.

The Old Man started walking, wondering to himself what it would be like to once more be at home, in his world. He was looking forward to seeing his friends and being with his daughter, his son and his grandchildren. And he was looking forward to spreading his new quilt on his bed and the rug on the floor of his study. In the distance he could see the wood through which he would pass. He quickened his step.

And then he stopped. The wood seemed to fade and then disappear, and a cold mist was covering the path so that he could not see where to go.

"Perhaps," he thought, "I have chosen the wrong day to do this. Perhaps I should wait for a better day?" And with that he turned around in order to walk back to his house. But when he turned the town was not there. In fact nothing was there, for the mist now fell all around him. He began to shiver and taking the rug from the bag and covering himself in the quilt, he sat down where he was, wherever that might be, and tried to find the shape of the wood in the distance. In a while he had lost any memory of what he had set out to do. He was frightened and could not move.

"I knew this would happen," said a voice behind him. "I knew you wouldn't get very far." The Old Man turned and there was the Housekeeper wrapped in a colourful and voluminous coat, with a hood pulled over her head to keep her warm. "Now look what you have done," she said. "You don't know where you are, you don't know where you're going, and now you've got mud all over your nice quilt. For goodness sake eat your honey and banana sandwich before you catch cold."

The Old Man felt into his bag and found his sandwich. And as he ate it his memory of what had happened returned. Or so he thought. He thought he could remember his journey through the wood; he thought he could remember arriving at the town; he thought he could remember the kitchen and the smell of toast; and he thought he could remember the work of the laundry and the rags hanging out to dry in the sunlit gardens. But now, since they all seemed to have disappeared, he was not sure.

"This is not such a good place to be," he said to himself. "And perhaps I have been dreaming and will soon wake up in my warm bed at home."

"It is no good sitting there wondering," said the Housekeeper. "And its no good hoping that this is all a dream. Either everything is a dream or nothing is. In which case you might just as well get on with it. Are you coming or are you just going to sit there?"

And with that the Housekeeper set off through the mist as if she knew where she was going, which she did. Frightened of being left alone, the Old Man picked up his bag, stuffed his rug and quilt into it, put on his hat, and followed her, making sure he kept her lumpy shape in sight.

Some time later, or so it seemed, as the mist began to lift and the warmth of the sun came to them, the Housekeeper and the Old Man found themselves walking along a pathway leading across marshland towards a river.

"Hold on a moment," cried the Old Man as the stride of the Housekeeper seemed to quicken. "Hold on!"

"I don't know why I bother with you," said the Housekeeper. "First you get lost and now you can't keep up. Is there anything in the least bit useful that you can do?"

The Old Man was beginning to think there was not.

"Well any way," said the Housekeeper, throwing off her cloak and letting it drift away towards the marsh, "we are nearly there now. I hope we haven't missed the tide."

At this point, the marsh gave rise to the river bank and when the Old Man had climbed up it he saw before him a curving river, and in the distance a wooden jetty with a boat moored alongside. It seemed as if the Housekeeper was taking him towards it. They followed the bank of the river until they came to the jetty and then the Housekeeper stopped.

"This is as far as I can go," she said. "If I go any further I will not be able to find my way home again. So it is now up to you. Either you come home with me or you continue your journey in this boat. But if you do, there is no way bay back. You will be gone forever from this In-between World. It's up to you."

And she stood there, her arms folded across her flowery dress and pinafore.

The Old Man sat down on the river bank and looked at the river, which was ebbing in the tide. He looked to see where the boat might take him if he set sail, but could only see that the river wound its way into the distance between the marshland. He wetted his finger to find the wind and felt it coming from the north following the flow of the tide. It seemed that everything was calling him to set sail.

"I have to go," said the Old Man. "I want to go."

"Of course you do," said the Housekeeper. "And you will find in your bag food and drink, and a spare pair of pants and socks. I must be off. Lots to do."

And with that she turned about and set off back along the river bank and across the marsh until he lost sight of her.

After a while, the Old Man slowly stood up and made his way down the jetty. He stood looking at the boat, thinking to himself, "If I go there will be no coming back. If I go there will be no coming back."

At that moment a small bird settled on the prow of the boat. It was dull, with a brown back and grey chest, but it had a yellow ring around each of its eyes. And on the river bank, on the other side of the river, was a large hare, its ears pricked up as if it was listening.

"Of course," said the Old Man, and he stepped into the boat, set down his bag, and hoisted the gaff sail. There seemed to be very little wind, but as soon as he had let go of the mooring and pulled in the main sheet, a breeze picked up from behind him and he was off.

With wind behind him and the tide beneath him, it was easy to sail the boat down river. And as he did so the hare ran along the bank ahead of him and the bird fluttered around him, sometimes taking a rest on the top of the mast. Opening his bag, he found sandwiches and a flask of tea.

"Excellent," thought the Old Man. "Excellent."

No-one knows how long it was that the Old Man sailed down the river. Some say a day or two and others a few years, but the tide was always ebbing and the wind was always behind him, there always seemed to be food and drink in his bag, and he was always in the company of the hare and the bird. He even managed to change his pants and socks, which were then immediately laundered clean and ready to wear. But however long it was, there came a day when the wind dropped and the tide stopped running. All the Old Man could do was drift and there, a short way off, stood another jetty on the other side of the river. The hare ran up to it and sat, as if waiting and the bird settled on the prow of the boat as if she was giving directions.

The Old Man took down the sail and as the boat bumped up against the jetty, he took ropes and secured it fore and aft to two large metal rings. Everything was very still and everything was very quiet. The Old Man felt both a sense of arrival and a sense of unease, wondering what would happen if he left the comfortable boat and entered into the land beyond the jetty.

"I think," said the Old Man to the bird, "I think I will just take a rest for while." And with that, he spread his rug on the floor of the boat and wrapping his quilt about him, rested his head on his bag and slept.

When the Old Man awoke, he found both the hare

and the bird sitting on the jetty, looking at him as if they had already been waiting for too long. He sat up, rubbed his eyes and yawned. Feeling into his bag he brought out a flask of tea and a banana and honey sandwich. This was his breakfast. Then he stood up and rolled his rug and quilt into his bag, looped its handle around his shoulders and across his chest and put on his hat. There on the floor of the boat was a hazel stick with a curled ram's horn handle. He picked it up, stepped out of the boat and onto the jetty. After walking a few paces along the jetty he looked back to see if the boat was properly tied to the mooring. But it was not there. Just the river, which had now turned, the rising tide now seemingly in full flow. No way back.

He left the jetty and, led by the hare and bird, found himself walking through beautiful countryside. Soon he was walking through gently rolling fields of corn, with well-kept hedges and small woods. The sky was a clear but gentle blue and everywhere he looked he could see bees and butterflies in the meadows of wild flowers. No-one knows how long he walked – some say a few hours and some say a few years – but after a while he saw in the distance what appeared to be an abandoned cottage, overrun by bramble and ivy and set within a garden surrounded by oak, horse chestnut and beech trees.

Somehow or other, the Old Man knew that this was where he was going. He felt a strange vigour running through his body and his steps lightened. He looked up into the sky, where the swallows were circling and saw both the sun and the moon. Indeed, he could see the stars and other planets sparkling in the deep blue of the sky – neither day nor night, neither moonlight nor sunlight, but a clear and shining brilliance everywhere.

Walking towards the abandoned cottage, he let his bag fall to the ground and he placed his stick against a hedgerow tree. He took off his hat and flung it into the air, where it whirled around and disappeared. He took off his shoes and his socks and left them by the path. And as he walked, the sun began to settle behind the cottage garden.

Soon he was there and although the garden was overgrown it was every garden he could remember – with valerian, cosmos, hydrangeas, cat mint, roses and a large buddleia, its blossom covered with butterflies and bees. There was an ancient apple tree and a drift of silver birch. He opened the garden gate and went in.

"So this is it," thought the Old Man to himself. "This is the ending."

Underneath the apple tree was a garden bench facing to the West. He sat down upon it and felt the day begin to close. Just before it set, the rays of the sun took on a new intensity and at once the Old Man was surrounded by a bright and wondrous light, the colour of eternity. Rising from the bench, the Old Man stood in the light, and as he did so he felt every part of his body breaking into the tiniest pieces and dropping away from him. Soon it was gone – all of it was gone, and with tears flowing from nowhere he let himself dissolve into the light. And as he did so he heard, as if in a whisper, the voices of all of those whom he had loved and who loved him.

It was over. And as he became at one, and the
sun sank below the horizon, the light gave way to
a deep and wonderful darkness. All was quiet.

In the garden, sat a hare and a small bird and on the
ground lay the Old Man's hat.

In my beginning is my end. In succession
Houses rise and fall. Crumble, are extended,
Are removed, destroyed, restored, or in their place
Is an open field, or a factory, or a by-pass.
Old stone to new building, old timber to new fires,
Old fires to ashes, and ashes to the earth
Which is already flesh, fur and faeces,
Bone of man and beast, cornstalk and leaf.
Houses live and die: there is a time for building
And a time for living and for generation
And a time for the wind to break the loosened pane
And to shake the wainscot were the field-
mouse trots
And to shake the tattered arras woven with a
silent motto.

In my beginning is my end. Now the light falls
Across the open field, leaving the deep lane
Shuttered with branches, dark in the afternoon,
Where you lean against a bank while a van passes,
And the deep lane insists on the direction
Into the village, in the electric heat

Hypnotised, in a warm haze the sultry light
Is absorbed, not refracted, by grey stone.
The dahlias sleep in the empty silence.
Wait for the early owl.
In that open field
If you do not come too close, if you do not come
too close,
On a summer midnight, you can hear the music
Of the weak pipe and the little drum
And see the dancing around the bonfire
The association of man and woman
In daunsinge, signifying matrimonie –
A dignified and commodious sacrament.
Two and two, necessarye coniunction
Holding eche other by the hand or the arm
Whiche betokeneth concorde. Round and round
the fire
Leaping through the flames, or joined in circles,
Rustically solemn or in rustic laughter
Lifting heavy feet in clumsy shoes,
Earth feet, loam feet, lifted in country mirth
Mirth of those long since under earth
Nourishing the corn. Keeping time,
Keeping the rhythm in their dancing
As in their living in the living seasons
The time of the seasons and the constellations
The time of milking and the time of harvest
The time of the coupling of man and woman
And that of beasts. Feet rising and falling.
Eating and drinking. Dung and death.

Dawn points, and another day
Prepares for heat and silence.

Out at sea the dawn wind
Wrinkles and slides. I am here
Or there, or elsewhere. In my beginning.

T. S. Eliot, *Four Quartets, East Coker, Part I*

LAST WORDS

There is a knowing in all that is. The bumble-bees know one thing and the sweet peas know something else. We know things, too.

All that is knows what to do. The bumblebees know what to do and the sweet peas know what to do. Sometimes we know what to do, too.

There is acceptance within all that is. The bumblebees accept their way and the sweet peas accept their way, too. We struggle to find our own way.

Which of us is wise?

Elsewhere is here and everywhere.

14663889R00140

Printed in Great Britain
by Amazon.co.uk, Ltd.,
Marston Gate.